The Shakespeare Handbooks

THE SHAKESPEARE HANDBOOKS

Series Editor: John Russell Brown

PUBLISHED

FORTHCOMING

The Shakespeare Handbooks

# Macbeth

John Russell Brown

First published 2005 by
PALGRAVE MACMILLAN
Houndmills, Basingstoke, Hampshire RG21 6XS and
175 Fifth Avenue, New York, N.Y. 10010
Companies and representatives throughout the world

PALGRAVE MACMILLAN is the global academic imprint of the
Palgrave Macmillan division of St. Martin's Press, LLC and of
Palgrave Macmillan Ltd. Macmillan® is a registered trademark in
the United States, United Kingdom and other countries. Palgrave is
a registered trademark in the European Union and other countries.

ISBN-13: 978–1–4039–3385–0 hardback
ISBN 10: 1–4039–3385–5      hardback
ISBN-13: 978–1–4039–2093–5 paperback
ISBN 10: 1–4039–2093–1      paperback

This book is printed on paper suitable for recycling and made
from fully managed and sustained forest sources.

A catalogue record for this book is available from the
British Library.

A catalogue record for this book is available from the
Library of Congress

10   9   8   7   6   5   4   3   2   1
14   13   12   11   10   09   08   07   06   05

Printed in China

# Contents

# General Editor's Preface

The Shakespeare Handbooks provide an innovative way of studying the theatrical life of the plays. The commentaries, which are their core feature, enable a reader to envisage the words of a text unfurling in performance, involving actions and meanings not readily perceived except in rehearsal or performance. The aim is to present the plays in the environment for which they were written and to offer an experience as close as possible to an audience's progressive experience of a production.

While each book has the same range of contents, their authors have been encouraged to shape them according to their own critical and scholarly understanding and their first-hand experience of theatre practice. The various chapters are designed to complement the commentaries: the cultural context of each play is presented together with quotations from original sources; the authority of its text or texts is considered with what is known of the earliest performances; key performances and productions of its subsequent stage history are both described and compared. The aim in all this has been to help readers to develop their own informed and imaginative view of a play in ways that supplement the provision of standard editions and are more user-friendly than detailed stage histories or collections of criticism from diverse sources.

Further volumes are in preparation so that, within a few years, the Shakespeare Handbooks will be available for all the plays that are frequently studied and performed.

**John Russell Brown**

# Preface

Like other authors of books in this series of Shakespeare Handbooks, I have set out to share my experience of this play in performance in a way that will help a reader to study the text in the element for which it was written. Having borrowed from other scholars to introduce what is known about the play's original publication and early performances, I become indebted in the commentary, which is by far the largest section of the book, to the many actors with whom I have worked on this play in rehearsal and performance. Their individual contributions are not recorded in footnotes because this would be an impossible task: I have no detailed or reliable recall of what happened over a number of years in different theatres and countries and I do not think any director or actor has that sort of memory. Besides, my intention is not to describe what has happened in the past but to help readers to envisage for themselves how the play can come alive in their minds, as on a stage, and reflect their own interests and experiences. This entails keeping in close touch with the words of the text to seek out all their many and various clues to how Shakespeare imagined his work in performance. I have tried to write the commentary as if I were preparing to direct the play all over again, only this time keeping an open mind about what the actors might do and the talents and experience they bring with them.

In a later section, four theatre productions and their leading actors are described in some detail and here, where possible, I bring other observers to comment and give evidence about what was achieved. In presenting the views of the play and its text by other authors, and when considering the cultural context in which Shakespeare wrote, I have quoted original sources wherever possible, as extensively as the size of this book allows. The longest passages quoted are from

Holinshed's *Chronicles*, which Shakespeare studied closely and used in creating the play's narrative and some of its dialogue. Very few editions quote this source at comparable length but it is offered here as a text to which a reader can turn when studying particular scenes or wishing to learn more about the play's origins.

The final section, on 'Further Reading', is not an extensive bibliography of scholarship and criticism but the means to follow up ideas arising from a reading of the play with this book in hand. It is also my opportunity to list books that I found particularly helpful in thinking and writing about this play. I am glad to acknowledge their influence but it is impossible to give details of my great debt to students and colleagues with whom I have studied Shakespeare and theatre in many forms, especially those in recent years at Michigan, Columbia and Middlesex Universities.

Thanks for help in the making of this book can, in a few respects, be more precisely directed. It owes much to other authors who are contributing to this series, with whom I have been able to discuss our common purpose and consider particular problems. It also benefits from a commission to write a series of articles on 'Landmark Productions of Shakespeare' for *Around the Globe*: by kind permission, the one on the Stratford production of 1955, with Laurence Olivier as Macbeth, appears in a modified form on pages 124–7. Another debt is to Anna Sandeman and, subsequently, Kate Wallis, the series editors at Palgrave Macmillan who have been untiringly helpful and supportive. Once more, my copy-editors, Valery Rose and Jocelyn Stockley, have been marvellously helpful and enlightening: I am much indebted to their assistance and my book is the better for it. For all this assistance, I am most grateful.

# 1 The Text and Early Performances

*The Tragedy of Macbeth* was probably written and first performed late in 1606 or early the following year, that is after *King Lear* and before *Coriolanus* and *Antony and Cleopatra*. In many ways it stands alone, its theme being Scottish and its Witches and their rituals unprecedented. The attention drawn to the innermost thoughts and feelings of the two leading persons is reminiscent of moments in earlier tragedies but now this is more intense and more sustained, a close focus that would not be repeated in later plays. The two silent entries of Banquo's Ghost are reminiscent of *Hamlet* and *Julius Caesar*, but its 'blood-boltered' appearance and the sighting of an air-borne and bloodied dagger are both innovations.

## The date of writing

The accession of James VI of Scotland to the English throne as James I in 1603 must surely have influenced Shakespeare's choice of a Scottish subject for the first and only time and also account for the play's references to James's descent from Banquo and his 'touching' to heal the 'King's Evil' or scrofula (IV.i.119–20 and IV.iii.141–59). Public interest in witchcraft during the early years of the century and the trial early in 1606 of conspirators who had tried to kill the king in the 'Gunpowder Plot' are also reflected in the play (see Chapter 3, pp. 93–4 and 94–5). Although *Tiger* was a fairly common name for ships (see, for example, *Twelfth Night*, V.i.58), the First Witch's curse on the 'master o' the *Tiger*' (I.iii.7–25) might well have been written sometime after 27 June 1606 when a ship of that name returned to Milford Haven in west Wales after a particularly hazardous voyage to the Far

East. Several small details in the play-text correspond to the later account of this *Tiger* published in 1625. Should this identification be correct, it would point to a date late in 1606 or early 1607 for the play's composition, to allow time for the news to reach London and become common knowledge.

Until recently it was widely believed that *Macbeth*'s Scottish theme, its allusions to James I and the likely date of its composition implied that the play had been written especially for a performance at court during the state visit of James's brother-in-law, King Christian IV of Denmark. It would have been one of the three un-named plays presented by the King's Men as part of the royal entertainment between 17 July and 7 August 1606. That its text is much shorter than those of other tragedies might have reflected the king's complaints when plays were too long, and the Banqueting Hall of Hampton Court having a smaller acting space than the Globe would have suited the intense intimacy of crucial scenes in this tragedy. When the Witches are said to vanish 'into the air' (I.iii.80) and Macbeth curses 'the air whereon they ride' (IV.i.137), opportunity would be given to use the stage machinery that was being developed for the elaborate masques of James's court. In these ways *Macbeth* was suitable for a royal occasion, but, when all is considered, late summer of 1606 is a most unlikely time for its première. An outbreak of plague had closed the city's theatres for seven or eight months from early June and so a command performance before James's royal guest would also have been the play's first performance at a time when public performances would normally precede presentation elsewhere. Moreover court records show that no expenses were incurred to pay for special masque-like effects on stage. *Macbeth* might have been written with eventual performance before James I in mind but we do not know whether this ever occurred.

Although numerous factors point to composition in the second half of 1606 or early 1607, the text that was published in 1623 quotes the first lines of two songs from Thomas Middleton's *The Witch*, a play written and performed by the King's Men sometime after 1609 and surviving only in manuscript until 1778. The text of *Macbeth* must therefore have taken its present form some years after it was written and, presumably, first performed. As we shall see, the introduction of songs was part of a more extensive revision that was probably to adapt the play for performance at the Blackfriars, an indoor play-house first used by the King's Men after 1609 and providing conditions more like those at court than those of the Globe. There is no means of knowing whether these changes were made with Shakespeare's involvement or approval.

The earliest documented performance was at the Globe theatre on London's Bankside on 20 April 1611. An astrologer, Dr Simon Forman, was present and wrote down his reflections in a diary, apparently taking care to check some details in the *Chronicles of England, Scotland and Ireland*, which had been Shakespeare's primary source (see Chapter 3 below, p. 99). This eyewitness account is some-times inaccurate or muddled and mixes fantasy with objective description (for example, no actors could have been seen riding horses 'through a wood') and yet Forman's account is often remark-ably close to the text. At one time considered a forgery, the diary was later authenticated and its account can now be taken as a thinking man's response to an early performance and, together with his simi-lar accounts of other Shakespeare plays, a rare and significant docu-ment.

In *Macbeth* at the Globe, 1610 [for 1611], the 20th. of April, there was to be observed first how Macbeth and Banquo, two noblemen of Scotland, riding through a wood, there stood before them three women fairies or nymphs, and saluted Macbeth, saying three times unto him, 'Hail, Macbeth, King of Codon [for Thane of Cawdor], for thou shalt be a king, but shalt beget no kings, etc.' Then said Banquo, 'What, all to Macbeth and nothing to me?' 'Yes,' said the nymphs, 'Hail, to thee, Banquo; thou shalt beget kings, yet be no king.' And so they departed, and came to the Court of Scotland, to Duncan, King of Scots, and it was in the days of Edward the Confessor. And Duncan bade them both kindly welcome, and made Macbeth [*sic*] forthwith Prince of Northumberland, and sent him home to his own castle, and appointed Macbeth to provide for him, for he would sup with him the next day at night, and did so. And Macbeth contrived to kill Duncan, and through the persuasion of his wife did that night murder the king in his own castle, being his guest. And there were many prodigies seen that night and the day before. And when Macbeth had murdered the king, the blood on his hands could not be washed off by any means, nor from his wife's hands, which handled the bloody daggers in hiding them, by which means they became both much amazed and affronted. The murder being known, Duncan's two sons fled, the one to England, the [other to] Wales, to save themselves; they being fled, they were supposed guilty of the murder of their father, which was nothing so. Then was Macbeth crowned king, and then he for fear of Banquo, his old companion, that he should beget kings but be no king himself, he contrived the death of Banquo, and caused him to be murdered on the way as he rode. The next night, being at supper with his noblemen, whom he had bid to a feast, to the which also Banquo should have come, he began to speak of noble Banquo, and to wish that he were there. And as he thus did, standing up to drink a carouse to him, the ghost of Banquo came and sat down in his chair behind him. And he, turning about to sit down again, saw the ghost of Banquo which fronted him so that he fell into a great passion of fear and fury, uttering many words about his murder, by which, when they heard that Banquo was murdered, they suspected Macbeth. Then Macduff fled to England to the king's son, and so they raised an army and came into Scotland, and at Dunston Anyse overthrew Macbeth. Observe also how Macbeth's queen did rise in the night in her sleep, and walked, and talked and confessed all, and the Doctor noted her words.

Dr Forman, an astrologer with a professional interest in prophecy and prodigies, was not an ordinary spectator but his account shows how the play's strong narrative made events seem to follow each other swiftly. Some moments of practical action or personal confrontation were sufficiently striking to remain vividly in mind. While the rights and wrongs of politics and personal morality were not considered a significant issue, instinctive reactions and strong feelings made clear impressions and were carefully noted. Lady Macbeth's sleepwalking is remembered as an episode standing apart and making unique demands for attention.

Four times Dr Forman notes that the action took place at night although performances at the Globe would have been given with actors and audience in whatever was natural light at the time. At certain moments the text calls for lights to be carried, as if these stage properties were intended to aid an illusion of darkness, for example in a stage direction when Fleance enters with his father, and several times in the dialogue when Banquo is murdered (II.i.0, s.d. and III.iii.9–19). But darkness in this tragedy is also evoked repeatedly in words and with sensuous images that must have fed the spectator's imagination; for example, in Lady Macbeth's:

> Come, thick night
> And pall thee in he dunnest smoke of hell . . .

(I.v.48ff.)

And Macbeth's:

> Come, seeling night,
> And scarf up the tender eye of pitiful day . . .

(III.ii.46ff.)

Or, with sudden and shocking brevity, when the sleepwalking Lady Macbeth cries out, 'Hell is murky' (V.i.35). These lines lodge in the mind today and it is reasonable to suppose they always did. However simply or grandly Macbeth was first staged and however vividly its horrors were enacted on the wide, uncluttered stage of the Globe almost encircled with audience, its most striking and compelling effects might have been its imaginary hold over the minds of actors and spectators. It seems to have been so for Dr Forman.

While we cannot recover early performances we know they were very different from any to be seen today. Women now play the female roles, as they never did at that time, and productions are carefully rehearsed, as they could never have been when a large repertory of plays changed daily at the public theatres. Both the crowded scenes and personal encounters would have been played with a constant regard for status and precedence that is unfamiliar to us. At a time when swords or other weapons were carried openly in the streets and about everyday business, the danger of being alone and unprotected was everywhere apparent and stage fights would have been managed with well-practised skill. The Witches' rituals would have been strange and uncouth, much as they are today, but, to a degree hard to estimate, they were also frighteningly and dangerously blasphemous. In the more enclosed spaces of the court, some private hall, or the Blackfriars theatre, darkness, violence and spectacle may have had greater effect than at the Globe but even there Shakespeare's subtle and innovatory handling of these matters is likely to have gripped a more surprised attention than they do in our technically well-equipped theatres. We can only speculate about the play's early staging but what is far more certain and timelessly effective is the way the dialogue repeatedly quickens the senses and frees the imagination of those who speak and those who hear: and this is especially so in this tragedy at crucial moments in the narrative, as the commentary that follows demonstrates. We shall also see how Shakespeare's handling of the on-stage action repeatedly directs attention to innermost thoughts and physical sensations.

## The First Folio edition

The sole original text was first printed after Shakespeare's death in the collected edition of his plays published in 1623 and known today as the First Folio. The manuscript sent to the printer was not in the author's handwriting but a transcript made from a manuscript that had been used in the theatre. It must have been carefully written because there are few serious errors or obscurities in the printed text. Indications of its theatrical origin are the consistency of character names and speech prefixes and a full provision of entries and exits, a few entrances marked earlier than necessary, as if warning actors to be ready, and a number of brief directions for music and sound. The printer's copy also contained the first lines of songs taken from Middleton's *The Witch*, as already noted, and probably other alterations and additions to Shakespeare's original text that were made with performance in mind.

The songs occur in episodes that follow two entries for Hecat. On the first, she reproves and instructs the Witches, declaring that she is 'mistress of [their] charms', and on the second, she approves of what they have done and commands a celebratory dance (III.v in its entirety, and IV.i.38–43). These episodes are not essential to the narrative or action of the play and could also have been late additions to the text. A speech for the First Witch that follows Hecat's second appearance could also be deleted without loss and, being written in a similar style, might also have been intended for the Witches' mistress (IV.i.124–31). Although the songs do not adequately fit the situation and are not in the idiom of the Witches elsewhere, Shakespeare might have been closely involved with the addition of Hecat or may have approved of it. She foresees Macbeth's future very accurately:

> He shall spurn fate, scorn death, and bear
> His hopes 'bove wisdom, grace, and fear.

(III.v.30–1)

And her warning that 'security / Is mortals' chiefest enemy' is a perceptive comment on much of the play. Shakespeare might well have approved of these additions, even if he had no hand in writing them, since, in his last plays especially, he changed the dramatic idiom markedly and introduced special effects for the introduction of gods and goddesses or for other persons whose functions are distinct from those of the main action.

Middleton might have been the author of Hecat's speeches as well as the songs, even though the witches in *The Witch* are very different from those in *Macbeth* and its Hecat is no goddess but the chief witch, who speaks in laboured verse (see pp. 57 and 63 below). As a younger playwright working for the King's Men at this time, Middleton is also a plausible author for other revisions that might have been made to the original text. When the Hecat scene was added, Act III, scene vi was probably moved from after the apparition scene (IV.i) to its present position in order to avoid two scenes for Witches following each other without a break. This change confused the narrative, causing Macbeth to say he will send to Macduff (III.iv.129) and then, before he returns the next day to the Witches, having an anonymous Lord report that Macduff has already turned Macbeth's messenger away and gone to England. More confusions are in the presentation of Lennox, and some unnecessary verbal repetitions may be the result of small additions being made or changes in the assignment of speeches. The passage about Edward the Confessor curing the King's Evil and being especially blessed by heaven (IV.iii.140–59) could also be a late addition: it is unnecessary for the narrative and easily detachable from the rest of the dialogue. By suggesting a power greater than that of other kings, the introduction of these lines would off-set and balance the power of Hecat, which is greater than that of the Witches.

The text's unusual brevity could also be a consequence of a revision that had to accommodate additional singing, dancing and spectacle for performances at court or Blackfriars. Any cuts made for performance should leave no trace but at least twice in the printed text more dialogue would greatly assist an audience's understanding. In the first Act, Duncan's naming of Malcolm as his heir and Prince of Cumberland is made abruptly, starting and finishing with a half-line of verse, and without naming any particular occasion (I.iv.36–43). Not a single verbal acknowledgement follows, except Macbeth's soliloquy, and this comes after other business and is spoken aside. Similarly, as part of the last speech in the play Malcolm's declaration that the Thanes of Scotland shall become Earls (V.iv.101–3) has an even greater brevity although this has large political implications that would find an echo in the creation of nobility by James I, which started early in his reign. This announcement, like Duncan's, begins and ends abruptly with half-lines of verse.

Scholars have been much concerned with these matters in recent years and, where immediately relevant, their debates will inform the commentary that follows. Without trying to identify a collaborator or dividing responsibility, the text will be treated as an accurate version of Shakespeare's play as it was performed by the King's Men a few years after composition when he would have been in semi-retirement and able to object if he had seen a need to intervene.

A further feature of the Folio text has to be borne in mind by readers and, more especially, by actors. More than for most plays, the verse-lining frequently calls for correction and often the nature of the dialogue means that this is a delicate task. At times, especially in the last Acts, speech is so fragmented that verse should, perhaps, slip briefly into prose and back again. Elsewhere a few words might best be printed alone in a line of type, as an incomplete verse-line indicating a silence or lengthy hesitation. Sometimes thoughts succeed each other strongly and two short lines should be shared as one between two speakers even though the verse would be irregular. Technical problems in the printing-house further complicated matters. The narrow columns in which the type for the Folio was set meant that many lines of verse could not be accommodated in one line of type and adjustments had to be made solely on that account. Adding to those difficulties, the manuscript had been marked so that two compositors could work on it simultaneously with pages taken out of their proper order; in consequence, the text sometimes had to be extended to fill more space, and at other times, rearranged to occupy less.

A simple transcription of the Folio can exemplify some of these editorial problems;

> Why do you make such faces? When all's done
> You look but on a stool.
> MACBETH    Prithee see there:
> Behold, look, lo, how say you.
> Why what care I, if thou canst nod, speak too.
>
> (III.iv.66–9)

Here A. R. Braunmuller's New Cambridge Shakespeare reads:

> Why do you make such faces? When all's done
> You look but on a stool.
> MACBETH    Prithee, see there! Behold, look lo! How say you?
> [*To Ghost*] Why, what care I! If thou canst nod, speak too.

George Hunter's New Penguin Shakespeare avoids an irregular line by printing 'Prithee see there!' as a half-line completing a regular verse-line begun with Lady Macbeth's 'You look but on a stool.' This tightens and sharpens the exchange and then leaves an incomplete line to indicate a pause before Macbeth turns to address the Ghost.

These few lines also illustrate how editors are drawn to modify the punctuation of the Folio. The New Penguin, for example, has no punctuation after 'what care I'. Comparison of any ten lines in any two modern editions is sure to give further examples of how a change of punctuation can change the effect, if not the meaning, of speech. Consulting a reproduction of the First Folio text will show the difficulties that would occur if a modern edition simply followed what the Folio prints; it will also show that some rejected readings might be defended. The accidents of printing and transcription with respect to punctuation mean that nothing in the Folio or any other edition carries the author's authority and a reader or actor should feel free to try further options as a means of exploring the values and effectiveness of the words.

## Note

*Macbeth* is quoted and referred to in this book from the New Penguin edition by G. K. Hunter, first published in 1967 and frequently reprinted. In common with other *Handbooks* in this series, all references to other plays are to the Oxford *Complete Works*, edited by Stanley Wells and Gary Taylor (1986), and the *Norton Shakespeare* that is based upon it with Stephen Greenblatt as its general editor (1997).

# 2 *Commentary*

## ACT I

### Act I, scene i

**1 to the end** Uniquely among Shakespeare's tragedies, and probably shockingly, the action starts with the noise of thunder, a lighting effect (strange, if not very noticeable, in open-air performances at the Globe), and three un-named and far from usual figures who are on the point of leaving. In *King Lear*, similar stage effects are hailed as the judgement of merciless gods but here the three Witches – so called only in stage directions and speech prefixes – accept the disturbance as their chosen element. And instead of eloquent or complex speech, the dialogue is in short, rhymed, and mostly monosyllabic verse, the metre having an insistent rhythm, as if from a drum. In arrangement the action is both formal and oddly abrupt: the first witch to speak asks questions, the second answers, the third completes the exchange with a more emphatic statement, rhymed with the preceding couplet. This sequence is repeated with shorter, more direct speeches but then, as Macbeth is named, three cries are heard from off-stage (or sudden on-stage reactions make them appear to do so) and the three Witches, without a word of explanation, come together to speak in unison, using an alliterative, rhyming, metrically irregular couplet of emphatic and yet mysterious import. The imperative 'Hover' at the beginning of the last line is free from the alliteration and monosyllables of the first.

For a reader, this short scene can pass easily and quickly but on stage its effect has been very varied. Accompanying action is often elaborate, with strange gestures and movement. The recurrence of thunder and lightning is either cued by the words or irregular in timing so that words have to accommodate to its louder, lingering sound. Speech may be ecstatic, crazed (even comic), unnatural in pitch, either struggling or at ease with the competing noise. The effect can vary between portentously prophetic and stubbornly self-centred. In view of later references to flight through the air and vanishing, productions with sufficient stage machinery have often had the three Witches fly off in different directions accompanied by sound effects or, a century and more ago, by music from a full orchestra. Stage lighting can show that the sun has already set and the air is heavy as thunder yields to fog. This short scene has attracted amazing scenic and directorial elaboration but, if the audience were ready to accept the Witches as malevolent creatures with a supernatural power to harm and prophesy, a simple, improvised staging could have uncanny effect.

Even on the wide, uncluttered stage of the Globe, surrounded by the audience and in full daylight, there were many ways of enhancing the scene and giving life to the text. Was speech given a clear, almost regular beat, its tempo slow with crucial words strongly accented? Was it accompanied by large, unnatural gestures or by contrary movements around or across the stage (see Ben Jonson's comment on p. 96)? Did the Witches move in unison, even when speaking independently? To what extent were their faces seen? Would a dance accompany the final couplet, involving a more powerful or more possessed state of being? Might the Witches have entered on the gallery, the upper level of the stage, so that they could disappear quickly and the next scene follow without interruption, as if these supervising presences have willed it to happen?

In some way the short scene must be emphatic, if not amazing. Otherwise the tragedy will start uncertainly and fail to catch attention. If the words are able to sink into the audience's minds, much will be at stake: a gathering on the point of dispersing, in foul weather and at the approach of darkness; and in the distance a confused yet decisive battle. From off-stage, alien demands break up the meeting and above the stage a storm rages; as the sun runs its course a filthy fog settles in the air. Whatever is about to happen, in a reader's or audience's imagination this event will be awesome and mysterious;

and yet in another way it is also simplistic, since 'fair is foul and foul is fair' and a battle will be 'lost and won'.

## Act I, scene ii

**1–24**　To the distant sound of battle, a king enters with his two young sons, a young thane (see 'my young remembrance', II.iii.59), and other un-named attendants. Their numbers and appearance contrast with what has gone before but, since the older son has recently been in danger (see ll. 3–40), they are all, like the Witches, unsettled and possibly on the move in search of safety. But this is not all: before anyone is named or any business of their own done, they meet with '*a bleeding Captain*', who appears unannounced. The attendants will at once be on their guard, on the lookout for other arrivals, while an audience that does not know the play is likely to believe that a battle has been 'lost and won' (I.i.4). Any uncertainty is quickly dispelled by the son's answer to the king's question and tension relaxes sufficiently for the soldier to tell his story, taking time for similes and parenthetic explanations, not unlike a messenger in ancient tragedies.

Everyone waits on his words as speech is sustained through extensive sentences, the syntax often strained, and verse-lining uncertain as if the wounded man were struggling to speak. But the sense is repeatedly concentrated in short statements with two strong syllables, reminiscent of the Witches' speeches: among them 'Doubtful it stood', 'But all's too weak', 'Till he faced the slave'. That last phrase is usually printed as an incomplete verse-line that indicates a pause, possibly to regain breath or master the pain of wounds, before it is followed with syntax of a longer reach that describes Macbeth's deeds. The Captain pauses again, giving more time for Duncan to respond in praise of his close kinsman. So, by now, the audience knows who everyone is and their relationships.

**25–50**　Now the Captain's words come closer than before to those of the Witches: first by speaking of the sun's progress and 'direful thunders', then by opposing fair 'comfort' to foul 'discomfort', sparrows to eagles, hare to lion. Before he is overcome by the pain of his wounds, a short verse-line indicates a pause after he has named Golgotha, another name for Calvary or 'the place of dead men's skulls' and the site of Christ's death on the cross. This reference, which is rare in plays of the period, precedes such a breakdown in speech that the wounded man has to be helped from the stage. While this is happening wordlessly, silence is broken by the entry of two more soldiers and again the king has to ask who they may be. Malcolm knows, as he did before, and Lennox sees promise of 'strange' news. After a brief and formal greeting, Ross pauses and Duncan takes charge with a further question. Rapidly attention has shifted: the king is again ill-informed and dramatic development again depends on reported off-stage events. Did Shakespeare intend to show Duncan to be a weak king, dependent on others (as in his source, Holinshed's *Chronicles*), or did he have unexpected entrances and information follow each other so neatly in order that the play's action should seem fated and, possibly, within the Witches' foreknowledge?

**51 to the end**    With his opening metaphors, and when he calls Macbeth 'Bellona's bridegroom', Ross speaks with the accent of ancient tragedy as the blood-stained captain had done but his speech is more controlled and more energized. It awakens a decisive response from the king and an order that is immediately accepted. The mood has been changed and forward movement clarified, all of which will be reflected in the attitude and postures of everyone on stage. Then in one line, the last before everyone leaves, Duncan speaks in the language of the Witches as if their prophecies were being fulfilled. Almost certainly the 'Thunder' that starts the next scene will overlap with the end of this one as everyone leaves the stage in relieved and buoyant mood.

### Act I, scene iii

**1–28**    After the 'haste' of the previous scene (l. 47), the Witches take their time, the First having leisure to make a detailed account of her doings. But after starting in blank verse with lines of ten syllables, the

threefold 'munched' and 'I'll do', with a reversion to rhyme and lines
of eight or seven syllables, have a shorter, stronger rhythm and are
closer to the idiom of the first Witches' scene. After the short line 17
when she sees into the future and delivers a curse, the speaker should
probably appear to be possessed. With 'tempest-tossed' she reaches a
climax in which her two sisters are probably caught up, the second's
intervention heightening the excitement before a small object is held
aloft as triumphant proof of this witch's power over human life.

**28–36**   A drum from off-stage is a sign of approaching soldiers and
interrupts proceedings at their most ecstatic. (Perhaps the drumbeat
is in the same rhythm that has been established by the words.) The
third witch takes charge, as she had previously, using two rhymed
lines of two beats each that change the nature of the scene. Without
a word the Witches join hands and start what appears to be a known
and fixed ritual with its own climax; physical movements are accompanied by six mostly rhymed, mostly iambic lines, all but the last of
seven syllables.

Some kind of incantation in unison seems necessary but what
happens on stage is not at all clear. Successive movement back and
forth in nine complete circles, which the words seem to require,
would take a great deal of time and could fail to hold attention unless
accompanied by very elaborate and strange gestures or business.
Possibly the witches move simultaneously, but independently from
each other, with different gestures and in contrary directions.
Perhaps the circles are indicated rather than enacted. 'Peace' (l. 36)
suggests a sudden cessation of movement and sound as the 'charm' is
completed and Macbeth and Banquo enter.

The three threefold movements of the charm echo and develop the
threefold repetition of words in both Witches' scenes this far into the
play. Many times more, an audience will be able to catch this emphasis, spoken and unspoken. Already, after three witches, three messengers have come unexpectedly to the king – the third, Angus,
remaining silent. Three familiar spirits have called silently for the
witches, the third being un-named. Very soon Macbeth will be hailed
three times. Later there will be three knocks at the gate of Macbeth's
castle and three murderers for Banquo and Fleance. Three apparitions

will appear out of the Witches' cauldron in Act IV, scene i, and in the fourth more elaborate 'show' eight crowned kings process across the stage, with Banquo's ghost making a ninth apparition.

A further clue to the staging of this scene is the first use of the phrase 'Weird Sisters', suggesting that at this point an audience should become more aware of their fateful implications. The phrase occurs in Holinshed, who glosses it 'the goddesses of destiny, or else some nymphs or fairies' (see p. 105, below). Because they were not in use before the early nineteenth century, *weird*'s modern senses, such as *odd*, *unusual*, or *fantastic*, are not valid here. (The Folio's 'weyward' and 'weyard' probably show that its compositors were puzzled by the unusual word and were influenced by the more common and less significant 'wayward'.) Although consistently called Witches in stage directions and speech prefixes, in spoken words the three are always weird sisters, sisters, or 'secret, black, and midnight hags' (IV.i.47). Only the First Witch uses the word 'witch' (I.iii.4) and then only when quoting a sailor's wife. For these reasons we may assume that when the charm is 'wound up' the Witches appear at their most authoritative and impressive, most like 'goddesses of Destiny'. Even if their audience does not believe in supernatural divination and influence over events, the Witches in the play must act here as if they possessed this power.

**37–51**  On entry, coming from a battle, Macbeth closely echoes the Witches from the first scene (l. 9) but it is less clear how he should enter and speak. His words do not seem to be part of ongoing talk nor does Banquo, his companion, answer or give any sign of hearing them. Perhaps he has stopped involuntarily, having sensed the Witches' presence: this could explain why he says what he does and how he says it; it could also motivate Banquo's question. Banquo is the first to give a sign of seeing the witches and yet Macbeth later says that they had 'stopped *our* way' (l. 76), as if he, too, had suddenly been made aware of them.

It is also remarkable that Macbeth remains silent while Banquo describes the Witches' appearance and actions, questioning their intentions. His interrogation will almost certainly hold an audience's attention until Macbeth breaks his silence with direct and compelling words, upon which he is hailed three times, the first a recognition, the others prophecies, the last so overwhelming in effect that Macbeth is startled and apparently afraid, an instinctive reaction described very differently later (see I.v.3–4). On seeing this, Banquo comes close to echoing the Witches' words as Macbeth's opening words had done (ll. 50–1). In this uncanny way, Shakespeare has given clear verbal signs of the tragedy's repeated concern with fate and free will and, at the same time, called for physical signs to augment what Macbeth is able or willing to say.

After the ritual of the charm and the simultaneous gestures of arms and hands in response to Banquo (see ll. 32–4), the Witches' repetitive greeting is also ritualistic. It should probably be given with at least the outward signs of demonic possession, or even hysteria. They probably encircle Macbeth and do some form of obeisance to him; Banquo would stand alone and out of focus. The three greetings and Macbeth's silent reactions, each one different from the others, can take plenty of time in performance, so heightening expectation and holding back the forward impetus of the play's action.

**51–68**    Banquo's 'fantastical' implies that he doubts the reality of what is happening and yet he is very aware of the implications of what he has heard and is at once competitive. With a steadiness quite unlike Macbeth's reaction, Banquo is careful not to submit to the Witches' claim to prophetic power (see also ll. 79–80). While more respectful, in some measure he, too, is afraid.

With shorter and less specific statements – yet threefold, antithetical and repetitive, and therefore still clearly prophetic – the Witches hail Banquo and then, with two lines addressed to both men, they are about to depart, probably with more ritual gestures. Immediately this alerts Macbeth, who briefly – peremptorily even – orders them back and demands to be told more.

**69–78**    Macbeth's thoughts have been hidden for much of this, his first scene, with the audience's attention directed towards his silences. Even now, while words come readily to make his point, he still does not tell all that he is thinking. Cawdor is not a 'prosperous gentleman', having been defeated in battle by Macbeth, and, while he vaguely dismisses any thought of kingship, very soon he will speak of an 'imperial theme' as if it were lodged in his mind (l. 128). Later, his wife knows he has the ambition to be crowned and is ready to help him attain it (see I.v.13–29). Here his speech has energy but also a careful restraint, as if he is eager to know more but determined not to say too much.

**78–88**  The Folio's '*Witches vanish*' can be managed without too much trouble if two of them leave, one at a time, while Macbeth addresses one of the others; the third and last can go off stage while he turns to face where he thinks one of the other two is still present. But such a manoeuvre needs directorial control to bring it off and that was not available in early performances, when perhaps a trap-door or smoke could allow them to vanish all at once on Macbeth's final 'charge'. Something amazing is needed to make sense of the next two speeches. Neither man can easily understand what has happened but, while Macbeth wants to hear more, Banquo goes on asking questions and beginning to doubt his own eyesight. A short line indicates a pause before Macbeth's statement (l. 83) immediately provokes another from Banquo, the implications of which Macbeth avoids.

At this crucial juncture, with the two generals probably searching each other's faces, Ross enters with Angus and, before greetings are exchanged, starts to deliver Duncan's messages. Some in the audience, knowing what he will say, may again sense the hand of fate in fulfilment of the prophecies.

**88–116**  Shakespeare omitted many details in Holinshed's account of the fighting with the rebellious Scots and their foreign allies, which Macbeth led with varied fortunes. Ross's account and the more direct contribution from Angus, speaking now for the first time, develop the mythical and heroic dimensions of the account given of 'Bellona's Bridegroom' in the play's second scene. If the audience thinks of Duncan when he is spoken of in this account of heroism and soldier-ship, he will seem weak in comparison – a king who keeps away from battle and is dependent on others, much as Holinshed describes his unfitness for authority and as his much longer narrative illustrates. In the play, no one voices this criticism but the action supports it: actors and audience are left to make any such judgement themselves.

Neither listener makes verbal response as the eulogy proceeds but when Cawdor is named, Banquo's brief aside breaks the focus and can express awe, fear, or possibly envy, according to the actor's choice and his sense of the person he plays. Now it is Macbeth who maintains control as he questions Ross and is answered by Angus. The four men alone on stage have great matters to consider that involve them each very differently. Some kind of stalling seems to be taking place as if instinct divides rather than unites them. At line 115, Macbeth replies with little more than a repetition of what he has heard but then, quickly, he breaks off at the start of the next line to speak what must be an aside that reveals the hidden 'prospect' of his secret thoughts (see Commentary on l. 73, above). As if immediately aware of possible exposure, he turns back to the messengers with brief and routine words of thanks. In return, they are silent, making, perhaps, some gesture of acknowledgement as the dramatic action continues to hang fire.

**117–25**   Somehow Macbeth manoeuvres Banquo so that they can talk without being heard by the others on stage. At the Globe there was plenty of space for doing this but such an initiative would be difficult to make without drawing unwanted attention: however staged, this is an awkward moment in which to share dangerous secrets. After the unusual word 'enkindle', which may be a conscious probe to discover Macbeth's intentions, Banquo changes the subject by turning to more general matters. Yet these also 'betray' deep consequences by developing his earlier 'Can the devil speak true?' (l. 106) and associating the Witches with supernatural and evil 'powers'. In his 'win us / our harm' and 'truths / trifles' an audience may catch an echo of the Witches' opposition of 'fair' and 'foul'. Banquo may be conscious of this since he is taking issue with them. After a silence indicated by an incomplete verse-line and with Macbeth now saying nothing, he turns to the messengers and, in contrast to Macbeth, calls them 'Cousins', a word that may mark his need for friendly contacts after thoughts of 'deepest consequence'.

Although '*They walk apart*' is an editor's addition to the Folio text,

'Cousins, a word, I pray you' indicates some movement of this kind. Alternatively, Banquo could move to the other two on stage, who are already standing apart because Macbeth had drawn Banquo aside at line 117. This would show that it is Macbeth who has an immediate and conscious need for secrecy, not Banquo, and would mark this difference clearly.

**126–47** Macbeth's first soliloquy starts with thoughts of kingship, the definite article probably showing that an 'imperial theme' has already occupied his mind. In Holinshed, he was brother to the king and (while Malcolm was too young to inherit) his natural heir but Shakespeare's handling of the story places him further from the throne so that thoughts of the crown do not arise from inheritance but from opportunity, his instinctive ambition, his wife's influence and, perhaps, from the Witches' instigation. Macbeth is familiar enough with these deeply engaging and dangerous thoughts to turn briefly and easily at line 118 to speak to those standing at a distance from him.

Once he is alone and his mind concentrated, thoughts are organized with statements followed by questions, the first (l. 130) bringing an echo of the Witches' 'fair is foul', the second showing him to be aware how greatly he has been affected physically. The actor will have to decide how far and how soon his outward appearance changes. Having heard the Ghost's message, Hamlet had to ensure that his 'sinews' would bear him 'stiffly up': in contrast, Macbeth says nothing of such a resolve. But almost as soon as he has used the word *murder* for the first time, he knows that his ability to function is threatened and that the very idea (or fantasy) of murdering has become more real than anything else. With dramatic focus almost entirely on him, Macbeth's inner thoughts and sensations are unequivocally the business of the tragedy. As he again echoes the Witches, his speech stops with an incomplete verse-line, as if he is shutting off more words.

Nevertheless, after a pause, Macbeth's soliloquy continues, only now with large gaps during which Banquo directs attention to him and finds excuses for his behaviour. The actor of Banquo will have to decide how fully he senses how dangerous and bloody his companion's thoughts have become; he might assume that 'new honours' are a sufficient cause for silence and unease. In fact, the thought that chance or fortune could fulfil the prophecy without his help is pulling Macbeth away from regicide. He succeeds well enough in this to finish with an upbeat though ambiguous couplet.

**148 to the end**   An appearance of normality returns, Banquo taking the lead in the transition. Macbeth addresses the messengers with careful, even conspicuous, courtesy: they are now '*kind* gentlemen' and he will acknowledge his indebtedness on every possible occasion. (Why is this so over-stated? an attentive listener might ask.) Yet as everyone is ready to leave the stage, Macbeth moves close to Banquo: he needs to know what he is thinking and has almost nothing to go on. His words are light enough to sound casual but 'weighed' and 'free' are not easy words in the context and the matter is brought to an end with abrupt and commanding speed. 'Come friends', on one level, is companionable and free, but this, too, could sound too brisk to be secure or comfortable. How the four leave the stage – how close they are together, at what speed, with what degree of decisiveness, suspicion, or relief – will set the seal on this scene according to the pitch and force of each one of the actors' performances and how they are interacting with each other.

## Act I, scene iv

**1–14**   The same persons enter with Duncan as in his first appearance in scene ii, but announced by '*Flourish*', instead of the military '*Alarum within*'. He is settled in his castle, giving an audience or sitting in counsel, everyone having removed outdoor and military clothing. Talk is careful and almost conversational, suitable for serious political business, until Malcolm starts to eulogize the traitor Cawdor. Like the Witches and Macbeth in the preceding scene, he also opposes fair and foul and, hearing this, Duncan acknowledges that this criminal had *seemed* entirely trustworthy and that his own judgement had been at fault. An audience may not catch this echo but then, at this very instant, as if fated, Macbeth enters: the audience will know very well that this thane is not be trusted, while it watches Duncan doing just that in his words of welcome. This step in the narrative is taken in a way that draws attention to deception and error, to what lies beneath appearances.

**15–36**   The four persons from the previous scene approach the king while silently expressing their subservience and loyalty. In return Duncan welcomes only Macbeth, greeting him warmly as a kinsman and praising him fulsomely, at the same time apologizing for his own inadequacy. Macbeth, whom the audience has just seen possessed and terrified by thoughts of murdering Duncan, now professes his total loyalty and duty to him. His courtesy is so careful and sustained that it could sound over-rehearsed. As 'Welcome hither' completes a verse-line a break could be taken in which the king embraces the victorious soldier, as he will later 'enfold . . . and hold' Banquo, whom he honours 'no less'. Banquo's response is far briefer, perhaps because he sees that Duncan has become almost overwhelmed with emotions of 'joy' and 'sorrow' (ll. 30–6).

**36–43**   Beginning and ending with a half-line, this passage brings many staging and performance problems. So much is effected so rapidly that the text may have been cut before being printed: the subject of the dialogue changes so abruptly at the start and finish of these lines that they could be omitted entirely and continuity maintained with only a tiny change or addition (see p. 8, above). As the text stands, there is no preparation for the announcement of Malcolm's new honour as Prince of Cumberland, and the consequences of this are not adequately explained. In contrast, Holinshed had stated clearly that Duncan is acting to secure the crown for Malcolm, who is too young to inherit should he die, in which event the crown would pass naturally to Macbeth as the reigning king's cousin and next in legal succession. Presumably Shakespeare decided not to have Macbeth so close to the throne but wanted to keep Duncan's attempt to secure the succession for Malcolm to give him an additional motive for immediate action.

Unfortunately for a modern audience, the words 'establish our estate' may not unequivocally entail succession to the throne.

Perhaps the technical words were better understood in early performances but most present-day directors have to provide stage business to signal what words do not. On being addressed formally, the
assembled company may take up positions according to rank, and
when Malcolm's new honour is announced everyone may kneel to
him. Trumpets may underline the official nature of the event and,
possibly, drum rolls. In ways like these, performance and staging can
clarify what is at stake although, after so many unambiguous
speeches, silent responses may have lost force and credibility.

**43–8**    Abruptly and briefly, as the text stands, Duncan invites
himself to Macbeth's castle and he humbly accepts and excuses
himself to make preparations and to soliloquize. These develop-
ments all take place with surprisingly little fuss; perhaps Macbeth
moves away during the king's brief response to be ready for speaking
aside. Paying homage to the new Prince of Cumberland can usefully
fill the time that Macbeth needs, continuing what remains of the
ongoing action without taking focus away from Macbeth. Each
person on stage may individually step towards the new heir to the
throne and swear personal loyalty.

**49 to the end**    Rhymed verse and many monosyllables show
Macbeth to be fully resolved on action as he leaves the stage alone.
However, only one verse-line runs without pause to its end and his
words continue to express fear; how strong that feeling is can vary
greatly with each performance and will affect his next entrance and
initial relationship with his wife. The scene winds up quickly but, for
the audience, with dramatic irony: Duncan leaves the stage, seeing no
danger but looking forward to the welcome and banquet, after which
he will be killed. Trumpets emphasize Duncan's confidence and
underline the irony.

## Act I, scene v

**1–12**    A greater shift in the action is hard to imagine: 'my wife' has
only once been mentioned before and without any great emphasis

(I.iv.47); and after military and political encounters between mostly independent men, here is a woman '*alone*' and reading a letter from her husband.

For an actor many questions arise. Why does she not hesitate – the punctuation gives no sign of this – and why enter alone to read a letter? If the words are spoken as part of an imagined reality, the actor is likely to decide that Lady Macbeth has read the letter previously and has now come to some more secret place to make sure she has understood every word. This way of playing the scene will help the audience to understand them too; perhaps it will notice (as she cannot) that Macbeth no longer mentions his 'fear' (see I.iii.50–1, 136 and I.iv.54) but writes only that he 'burned with desire'. The phrase 'my dearest partner in greatness' is unusual, suggesting an affection-ate and equal relationship between two persons who possess politi-cal power. (See also 'lay it to thy heart', with which the letter ends.) At this stage in the play's action, the phrase could mean that they have shared thoughts of kingship: very soon, 'wrongly win' (l. 20) suggests that they have together considered murder or some other crime to win 'the golden round' of the crown (ll. 25–8).

**13–28**   The soliloquy starts ecstatically because the Lady has been transported 'in the instant' to 'feel' that their ambition has been fulfilled (ll. 54–6). The actor needs a strong imagination to carry this off so soon after a first appearance on stage, but full confidence is not demanded at first. After the first exclamations, she speaks of her own thoughts and uncertainty plays its part. Line 14, although printed as one verse-line, could be spoken as two half-lines with a silence between them allowing silent thought to take over. Then the solilo-quy moves steadily forward as she considers her husband's ability to act upon their agreed plan; it culminates in a determination to empower him with her own 'spirits', at which point she is, again, 'transported' (see l. 54) in imagination to a royal future.

**28–36**   The messenger enters at just the appropriate time, as if fated. To warrant and make sense of 'Thou'rt mad to say it,' Lady Macbeth must instinctively misinterpret the simple message, imagin-ing that her husband is the king who comes that very night. Then, in half a line, she steadies herself and finds a question that will cover up her outburst. In any simpler reading of her response, the initial exclamation would lose credibility: there is no other reason why she should call the messenger 'mad'.

**36–52**   Her imagination is again at work. She becomes acutely aware of the intended murder. Hearing a raven and calling on spirits, she knows she has to lose the conventional tenderness of her sex and any thought of consequences, otherwise she dare not see the 'wound' she is ready to make; rather than that, she wants the darkness and stench of hell to inhibit her consciousness. So much her words imply but, in performance, much is left to the actor. Is she fully aware of what she has determined to lose, or is she too reckless for that? Does she, in some ritualistic way, offer herself or at least her breasts to agents of darkness and hell, either kneeling in submission or standing in proud committal? Is there any hesitation or mark of tenderness as she commits herself and begs for her milk to be turned to bitter gall? Does she *see* the 'keen knife' and *feel* its sharp edge? She may so change that she alters in presence and potential before our eyes. As Macbeth is about to enter, she imagines the murder itself and hears a voice from 'heaven' or from God, as it might have been if theatres did not risk being censored for using that word. If the actor imitates the voice that Lady Macbeth hears, an audience may also believe that it is actually speaking, like the one heard by King Kenneth in the episode in Holinshed (see pp. 102–3 below) that Shakespeare uses later when Macbeth has 'done the deed' (II.ii.14, 35–44). The imagined voice is the climax of the speech, at which very moment her husband enters.

   To what extent can any actor respond to all the demands of these words? When writing this solo scene, it is very possible that Shakespeare's imagination had moved beyond the practicalities of performance.

**52–68**   After the exultant awareness of her greeting, they both speak with amazing and thrilling brevity. Following the tenderness implied by 'My dearest love' (at which time they may have embraced), the simple words 'Duncan comes here tonight' are a reminder of the crime they have purposed to undertake together. If less than this is implied, why do the next three speeches follow and what other meaning can they have? Macbeth's 'Tomorrow, as he purposes' may suggest some hesitation but, if so, Lady Macbeth's answering words silence such a thought.

The incomplete verse-line 58 indicates a pause before she continues with practical concerns. If they are close together or have remained in an embrace, she will have to move back to see the look of horror and fear that is on his face. Now she is in control and taking charge of events. She avoids speaking of murder – that is now the 'night's great business' – but she is ready – and may intend – to kill Duncan herself (as she had imagined at line 50). In some performances she is clearly possessed by the 'spirits' she had called upon moments before, in much the same way as the Witches have been possessed.

**69 to the end**    His wife had concluded with a confident couplet, in contrast with which Macbeth's short counter-statement – 'We will speak further' – could either signal agreement or insist that he is not yet ready to act. Either way, the future is uncertain and, hearing this, she again reassures him with a couplet and follows that with her own short line, taking full responsibility for the action.

By saying nothing further in response to her, Macbeth ensures that the scene ends ambiguously unless it is resolved in performance by the way they react to each other physically as they leave the stage. An audience has been led to watch closely so that the smallest details of the two performances can register. She may lead or, perhaps, draw him off stage; or they could go together as he accepts her leadership; or neither may appear sure of the other. Perhaps an audience should be left in doubt as to who is the stronger 'partner' at this stage in the play so that interest in its development is whetted and attention still further sharpened.

## Act I, scene vi

**1–9**    After the intense focus and fraught nature of the previous scene, a sweeping contrast is achieved with a stage more crowded than before, arrivals after a long journey, and talk about the weather and the host's castle. All seems set fair on stage when everyone in the audience knows very well that it is not. Banquo elaborates on the moment by speaking of martlets [*house martins* or *swallows*], which, by nesting on the outside of buildings, were held as auguries of peace for those places. Perhaps he is aware of the irony of this: he knows that all is not entirely safe because Macbeth has been 'enkindled' to take Duncan's crown (I.iii.119–21) and may, like the audience, be thinking of danger, political turmoil and, possibly, God's providence (see II.iii.126 and commentary).

The '*Hautboys*' of the Folio's stage direction are not suitable instruments for travellers, and may be intended to accompany Lady Macbeth's entry at line 10. Nor are '*torches*' needed in daylight: this stage direction probably applies to the persons who carry these properties and will use them later. A large number of persons are needed to give the impression of a royal retinue and welcome.

**10 to the end**    Duncan has not been listening closely to Banquo: he sees Lady Macbeth at once, comments as she approaches, and addresses her before she can speak. Momentarily some in the audience may wonder why she is welcoming the king and not Macbeth himself; Duncan seems to have expected the master of the house (see l. 20).

Lady Macbeth may remain kneeling while she heaps up phrases expressing her loyalty and welcome. Few in the audience will fail to understand that 'fair' words hide thoughts that are quite contrary: she is so far from a 'hermit' who prays for Duncan's well-being that she may over-step what is acceptable; possibly, she is enjoying her own performance. While noting Macbeth's absence and 'his great love' for his wife, the king continues in his own courteous and complimentary mode, with promise of further honours. He may also be responding to a heightened sense of opportunity that Lady Macbeth cannot entirely hide. 'Give me your hand' may be Duncan's way of indicating that she may rise at this point or in other ways cease to show submission to her king. Some editions (including the Penguin) direct Duncan to kiss his hostess on this cue but the words could be no more than a courteous apology for entering the castle gates alongside his hostess, rather than ahead of her as precedence required.

## Act I, scene vii

**1–28**   Music, lights, and a sequence of entries and exits with food
and all the paraphernalia for a state feast, form a wordless interlude
representing lavish hospitality and a celebration of the king's presence. The sound of guests might also be heard in the background.
Then, without warning and shutting a door behind him for greater
secrecy, Macbeth enters alone. An audience not knowing the play are
likely to be taken off-guard and puzzled until he speaks his first line,
its monosyllables suggesting a slow delivery despite their obviously
urgent implications.

Because the second line has more syllables than a regular
pentameter, it might better be printed as two incomplete lines, indicating a pause before Macbeth brings himself to name 'the assassination'. As he thinks of consequence and judgement, ideas and phrases
are repeated and regular syntax broken so that hesitation and
forward impulse seem to work together in conflict until line 20,
which again may be taken as two incomplete verse-lines that indicate
a pause. He continues in a more reasoned, less hesitant manner until
thoughts of Duncan raise contrary considerations and feelings:
sentence structure lengthens as powerful, luminous and kinetic
images start to arise freely, as if unbidden, even as the 'horrid deed' of
intended murder comes again to mind. Towards the end of the soliloquy, violence and pain begin to dominate. The actor will have been
stretched and torn by the conflicting sensations he has been required
to represent and is likely to look exhausted, much as Macbeth must
be.

In performing or reading the play, Macbeth's praise of Duncan
may well be unexpected and even seem undeserved. As king he has
been mistaken on several crucial issues, has held back from battles
waged in his name, and at all times has been reactive, rather than
active and strong. In Holinshed he is repeatedly faulted for being too
soft and pious to be an effective king (see pp. 103, 104, etc.) and something of this may remain in Shakespeare's treatment of him. Much
will depend on the actor and how he plays the kingly role, the play-
text allowing scope for both meekness and authority. Macbeth may

paint him fair in compensation for being 'foul' in his private thoughts.

**28–61**    As she enters, Lady Macbeth says nothing but he senses her presence at once. Their short phrases are terse and their questions are likely to heighten tension because so much depends on their mutual trust. Unable or unwilling to answer her second question, Macbeth changes tack and gives his new decision in a single line, speaking of 'we' before weakening its effect as he fails to give the true reasons for the reversal of plan – neither horror at what he was about to do nor fear of judgement, having done it. His wife cuts through this, first with scornful questions about his strength of mind and then with a short, sharp judgement on the nature of his love. With lengthening and strengthening rhythms, more questions follow that mock his resolve and finish by calling him a coward and likening him to a 'poor cat' who wants to eat fish but is afraid to wet its feet. Being unable to listen to more, Macbeth interrupts and then, very clearly, states his case, based, now, on natural human dignity. The result is that for the next twelve lines he is silent while she taunts him for not being the person she had believed that he could be: time and circumstances have brought it about that they can act as they had agreed and, yet, he does nothing: 'their fitness now / Does unmake you'.

He must have stood watching and listening all this time, hardly moving. Now he responds by stiffening or moving away; perhaps an instinctive cry of protest escapes him, as if he were unwilling to take more punishment. Some such physical, wordless reaction tells her to change the grounds of the argument and, in an instant, she challenges him to equal herself in courage and resolve: she would kill her own infant at her breast if she had sworn to do so as he has sworn to kill the king according to their pact. He has followed every word she has said and is now ready to take a step forward. They have become so in tune with each other's thoughts that very simple and repetitive words serve: 'If we should fail?' – 'We fail!'

Editors disagree about what happens here and so arrange these speeches and their punctuation very differently; and individual actors respond differently, too. She may prevent him saying more by a further question, 'We fail?' Alternatively, she accepts the risk without argument, making a blunt, mind-stopping statement: 'We fail.' The two speeches are sometimes printed as one line on their own, the previous line starting, as in the Folio text, two syllables earlier than in the Penguin edition: this arrangement indicates a silence before or after Macbeth speaks. Sometimes 'We fail!' is a line on its own, indicating a long silence before or after it is spoken. Whatever the timing of these speeches, he may have moved towards her and, with her first two words and the encouragement that follows, she may draw him closer, sure now of success and ready to offer detailed plans for managing the murder (ll. 61–72). However these lines are timed and played, he is ready to 'leave all the rest' to her, as she offered earlier (I.v.71). If he moves towards her entirely of his own accord, he will not seem so much in her power as the words alone suggest. For the second time, the audience has been led to observe and listen closely to the actors on stage: the development of the action depends on their mental and physical relationship, at a level of consciousness deeper than words.

**62 to the end**     He is silent again as she takes time to picture their victims, speaking now of what 'you and I' (l. 69) can perform: it will be a shared performance – that is how she envisages the murder – and she finishes by speaking of 'our great quell': that is, their shared and notable act of killing or suppression of all opposition. His immediate response is to admire her 'undaunted' spirit that would nourish males – expressed, perhaps, with a reference back to her invocation of motherhood (ll. 54–6); his next step is to accept her leadership and contribute to the plan. Finally, the balance between them is drawn into question again: he declares himself 'settled' and speaks of his own actions; he then leads the way off stage, accepting the advice she gave as they left together on an earlier occasion (I.v.69–70). This time she is silent and how close they are, physically, mentally and emotionally, once more is of great importance if we wish to estimate the meaning of his words and their consequences as the play proceeds.

At the close of the tragedy's first Act, attention has been focused closely on the two protagonists and their childless marriage, a relationship that depends on listening as well as speaking, on physical presence and sexual attraction as well as words, and on what is thought but not spoken. Every actor will find his or her own way through this scene and it is unlikely to remain exactly the same from one performance to another. Besides, the tragedy depends here on such fine tuning that performance is also bound to develop in response to each audience. What is happening is mostly obvious, but what its causes and its effects are, every actor and audience will have to discover for themselves.

# ACT II

## Act II, scene i

**1–11**  As the stage empties and murder is imminent, a boy enters carrying a lighted torch. At the Globe Theatre, in daylight, this would signal that it was night time, an impression reinforced by talk of the moon that had set and a starless sky. The boy is not named but Banquo follows close behind and they speak with the familiarity of father and son, the 'sir' of line 2 being the usual form of address within families, even in private. The boy will not easily receive a sword and then another object (probably a sword belt) as required by the text, since he is already holding a torch, so there may well be some fumbling.

Everything else is still and silent so that Banquo's words and, more especially, his prayer can seem to arise from a deep self-consciousness: there is no other cause to speak as the play's forward action is in abeyance. The actor may choose to make 'accursed thoughts' refer to his own future in the light of the Witches' prophecies or to forebodings concerning Duncan, now that he is lodging in Macbeth's castle. Alternatively, allowing for the prohibition about dealing with religious matters, Banquo can be brooding, more piously and in more general terms, on Christian teachings with regard to man's original sin.

A sound and then two figures with a torch break the reflective mood and so Banquo takes back his sword to challenge the unknown newcomers. With his recognition of Macbeth, comes a question that could simply be good manners or might be a mask for serious suspicion. In present-day productions, the darkened stage can easily add to the mystery of this episode but the original staging in daylight with the actors totally visible might have given a sharper sense of their shared yet contrasted responses to danger.

**12–32**    When he hears of Duncan's gift, Macbeth has other thoughts that lead him to reply with an allusion to his own discourteous departure from the banquet before his royal guest had retired. Very briefly Banquo dismisses his unease only to open up the momentous matters that lie beneath all other words. Both speak guardedly and yet with apparent unconcern and openness. The mood has changed and nothing is 'leaden' now for either of these two, who had found each other walking alone in the castle late at night. Words are cunningly used – 'some truth . . . entreat . . . some words . . . that business . . . kindest leisure . . . cleave to my consent . . . honour for you' – until Banquo speaks on his own account (ll. 26–8), whereupon Macbeth closes the subject by reverting to ordinary courtesy. As soon as Banquo and Fleance leave, Macbeth starts the action for which he had entered, not knowing he would meet anyone.

**33–48**    Escaping the pressures he has felt by taking action and sending a directive to his wife, Macbeth is no sooner alone than he is gripped by a hallucination. For actors, this is a difficult transition but, when credibly achieved, it opens up a further dimension to the play in which the subconscious intrudes upon the real and threatens sanity. The audience should not only hear that he sees the dagger but should also be able to *see*, in some palpable way, that he sees it. Some in the audience will believe that he is on the brink of madness and so, perhaps, may Macbeth himself. Madness and fantasies are closely linked in Shakespeare's plays: for example, when Hamlet sees his father's ghost and Gertrude does not, she at once declares, 'Alas, he's mad' (III.iv.96) and he has difficulty in proving otherwise.

At first, Macbeth struggles to understand by asking himself questions, finding words and seeking explanations for what he sees, and trying to clutch the phantom dagger and then drawing the real one that he is wearing. The incomplete verse-line (41) indicates a silence before his attention is again fixed on the phantom, which is now covered with blood. In all probability, physical as well as mental effort is needed to deny its existence, on the suddenly compact and forceful, 'There's no such thing' (l. 48).

**49–61**   Recognizing that what he is about to do has tricked his eyes leads him to sense that he is alone and, as if drugged, not fully awake. The dagger proves to be the least of what he experiences: he is trapped in a world of witchcraft and is the epitome and personification of murder as he moves stealthily and lustfully, but only half alive, towards the act that so recently appalled him. After a moment's call for silence, horrifying though that is, he knows that now, at last, he must act and that more talk is useless. At this very moment, the bell that his wife has struck is heard off stage and summons him.

**62–4**   As he is about to move, Macbeth suddenly sees himself doing what he knows he has to do, like an automaton, and immediately he thinks of his victim, wishing to save him from being conscious of what is about to happen. This final couplet runs easily towards its conclusion, seeming to assume an ultimate judgement in which the fair will be eternally blessed and the foul forever tormented. Alternatively, and far more easily, Macbeth may be taking courage by mocking the conventional piety of his victim, as Shakespeare's earlier Richard the Third repeatedly does. For the actor, this is a crucial choice to make at a significant moment in the tragedy when Macbeth's exit from the stage draws a very concentrated attention from his audience.

### Act II, scene ii

**1–13**   As Macbeth leaves in one direction, his wife enters from another. In contrast to his now purposeful movements, she is extraordinarily alive and responsive to an unexpected noise – unless, perhaps, she only imagines the 'shriek' of the 'fatal bellman' that she welcomes. She seems to have no precise purpose in being here, except to be as near as possible to what is happening off stage. Her senses are heightened, enabling her to visualize her husband at the scene of the murder they have planned and to be satisfied with the effectual part she has played in it. When he unexpectedly cries out, she is again alert, this time afraid that he has failed to do what is required. Her phrases, and probably her movements, have become briefer and more urgent now, her manner distracted and, perhaps, wild. Yet, in midst of her fear, she remembers a quite different reaction that is special to herself (see ll. 12–13).

Thought of her father could be passed over quickly, like many of her reactions at this time, nothing mattering now but success by any means. Or it could express feelings that would otherwise be hidden: frustration at her own weakness in failing to take matters into her own hands; a surge of deep feelings not recognized earlier in the ongoing course of events; a sudden recall of Duncan's appearance in sleep that makes her think in a new way about her own part in his murder.

At just this moment, Macbeth enters holding the bloody daggers and all other thoughts vanish out of her mind: she greets him as her 'husband', a word she does not speak elsewhere in the play. Whatever sensation this expresses will be a key to the actor's entire performance: relief, satisfaction, pride, or warmth of feeling towards him. If she has seen the expression on his face or if he is physically racked by insecurity or pain, her greeting could express alarm, reproach, or encouragement. How words and actions will be played at this moment cannot be predicted when entering a theatre to see the play. Study of the text will be of very little help because the two words are so ordinary out of their context. But when their time comes in a performance, the manner of uttering them should have become inevitable and uniquely expressive in a way that is suitable to the performances of both actors from the start of the play until this highly fraught moment.

The range of possible physical enactments is as huge as that of verbal interpretation. The recent New Cambridge edition directs Macbeth to enter where it is marked in the First Folio, immediately after his wife's '. . . live or die', half way through line 8, and it places a question mark after 'husband'. The editor explains in an extended note that the confusions and hesitations of both persons in this staging are due to the (imaginary) darkness on stage and their inevitable uncertainties and anguish. The scene is tense and neither person on stage may fully comprehend what is happening, but a question here would be unproductively difficult for the performers to act and the audience to understand.

**14–21**　'I have done the deed' can be said with many different implications, at varying pitch, volume and emphasis, but the monosyllables suggest a slow delivery. Whatever these first words express, between exultation and defeat, in what follows both speakers are so directly and simply involved with listening in near-silence and with total involvement that all ambiguity will tend to vanish. An audience is likely to be caught up in their palpable tension and expectancy. At line 20 Macbeth sees his bloody hands, which neither of them has seen or, at least, mentioned before – although an audience might have noticed them as soon as he entered. The short line indicates a pause before he speaks and, after this acknowledgement, the text gives no indication that he even thinks of doing anything about the blood. But he does continue to be appalled at the sight and he will come to imagine that the blood-stained hands 'pluck out' his eyes (l. 59). His wife, however, immediately and curtly reproves him.

**22–43**　The sight of blood has taken Macbeth's mind back to the place and circumstances of the murder and, although he is 'afraid to think' what he has done (ll. 51–2), he vividly relives it. He is either begging for sympathy or seeking to understand his helplessness and compulsion, or to find their cause. The second time his wife tries to bring him back to rational thought, he stops speaking for a moment, only to ask, for a second time, why he had been unable to join in the grooms' dying prayer. When she warns him of madness (l. 34), he starts to tell of the nightmare voice he heard. Holinshed, when recounting the incident from which it was taken (see pp. 102–3, below), assures the reader that this was the voice of 'almighty God', and Macbeth should, perhaps, make clear that this Christian authority lay behind the message by using some ritualistic gesture or posture. When Claudius finds he cannot pray in *Hamlet* (III.iii.36–71), the Christian associations are unmistakable.

In whatever way he speaks of the voice, it has awakened memo-
ries of peaceful days when 'labour' was followed by 'balm' and
nourishment (ll. 36–40): for a moment his agony abates or is
forgotten and another vista of well-being opens in his mind and in
those of the audience. (Analogous transference to an ideal world
has already occurred when Macbeth remembered Duncan, and will
recur when he faces defeat in the fifth Act; see the Commentary
on I.vii.16–25 and V.iii.24–6.) Asked what he means, he may feel
his entire body weakened, inwardly sickened and distraught, as the
full horror returns. The repetitions of ll. 41–3 ring ominously and
helplessly.

**44–57**    With question, encouragement and instruction, Lady
Macbeth takes the initiative so firmly that he does not or cannot
move; or, perhaps, he moves further away from the door through
which he entered. With scornful reproach, she demands to be given
the daggers. This much could hardly be more clear: she has decided
to act alone and take control of the situation. But does he *give* the
daggers to his wife or does she have to take them? Is this crucial
action over in a moment or does it occupy much of the time that she
continues to speak, so that only with 'if he do bleed' is she ready to
leave?

The extent to which Lady Macbeth is giving herself courage by
talk of 'pictures' and a 'painted devil', as opposed to continuing to
reprove her husband, can only be determined in performance. She
can seem completely isolated from him by now but, possibly, the
relationship between them is sufficiently close for the two to act as
one when so much is at stake. The moment has been frequently
painted and photographed because it encapsulates the effect of both
performances. The sentence on which she leaves (or after which she
leaves) can vary between cool thought, insisting that all is going
according to plan, and a hasty improvisation of the moment, the pun
on 'gild' and 'guilt' either speaking for her fears or expressing an
access of mental as well as physical energy. Aware on entry that
events had made her 'bold' (l. 1), her speaking of boldness then and
her demonstration of it now suggest that, despite her hesitation on
seeing Duncan to be like her father, she has been wanting to take over

the murder; that could be why she is so soon impatient with her husband. What is most certain in this scene is that Shakespeare has ensured that both protagonists are involved with the murder and, at the same time, are discovering the very basis of their beings and mutual relationship.

**57–63**   The first of many knocks from off-stage, representing arrivals at the castle gates, is as fatefully timed as any of the many coincidents of the tragedy's plotting; this was Shakespeare's addition to the sources, a sign of his concern with the operation of fate in presenting this deeply personal story. The sound, unlike others in the scene, is immediately recognizable, which argues that it should bring ordinary living to mind as well as being a cause for alarm: it brings a more rational awareness to Macbeth, even as it 'appals' him. Horror at the blood on his hands opens up his mind to visions, expressed with images that suggest overwhelming sensation and vast perspectives in a mind that is also precise and complex. Macbeth, alone on stage, holds attention until his last four monosyllables still further sharpen perception and, simultaneously, baffle understanding.

**64 to the end**   The preceding incomplete verse-line suggests that Lady Macbeth enters after a silence, during which Macbeth is 'lost . . . in [his] thoughts' (ll. 71–2). Or she may enter as he finishes speaking and the sight of her reddened hands at once transfixes him. She is immediately resourceful, reproaching and instructing him in what he should do, her words punctuated by the knockings which, when he has found his voice again, become ominously threefold (see Commentary, pp. 15–16 above).

The scene does not end with a couplet but with Macbeth's three separate exclamations, each marking a further access of understanding. The regret of the third cry, if played with total belief and at full power, throws the entire progress of the tragedy into question, in Macbeth's mind and in those of the audience. In performance this is usually the time when she insists on her bloody hands grasping his bloody hands and drawing or leading him off stage.

## Act II, scene iii

**1–18**  Audiences are invited to laugh when a comic actor enters immediately after the terror and deep-seated drama of the previous scene. The Porter speaks in prose and reluctantly stumbles on stage to do his duty after a long night's drinking, perhaps still struggling into his clothes, as the off-stage knocking continues. As a comic performer, he can speak for himself and also be conscious of the theatre audience for whom, in early performances, the subjects he talks about were ones they could have encountered in their own lives; speculation and financial disaster, physical sweating and fashionable clothes, all presented with increasingly bawdy suggestion. Except for a notorious traitor and would-be arsonist (see p. 93, below), all the persons the Porter imagines to be knocking at the gate could have been met on the streets of contemporary London and do not belong to a Scotland of five centuries earlier.

Dramatic perspective and subject matter have changed radically, even though the audience had been left waiting to know more of the consequences of Duncan's murder. However, at the same time, and more obviously in keeping with what has gone before, the Porter also imagines himself to be stationed at the gate of Hell, assisted by the devils of Christian tradition and Holy Writ (see pp. 98–9 below), with 'the everlasting bonfire' in prospect. So, while a sense of escape and relief is assured, at the same time the moral and religious implications of the main story could be brought as much to the minds of an audience as the more usual and easier pleasures of a clown's performance.

Much depends on how this episode is performed. Today it is likely to raise little laughter because the dialogue is no longer topical and its verbal meanings have become obscure; its effect will mostly depend on physical comedy and the clown's stage personality and reputation. If the Porter fully imagines the people he describes, he can 'see' them passing across the stage or imitate their behaviour with comic exaggeration. Some clowns are good at portraying terror, or even death itself, and they would find scope for that talent in the devils and roasting in hellfire. However it is played, after its release into prose and comedy, this episode concludes with a moralizing comment and some recurrence of foreboding. The sound of knocking can be ominous, even if reaction to it is laughably indignant.

**19–39** As he opens a door to the stage and reminds new arrivals of his customary tip, the knocking ceases and the Porter is reproved for taking so long to answer the summons. In reply, a comic digression on the effects of drink offers him opportunity to play with notions of desire, equivocation and disappointment, laced with more obvious bawdy innuendo. Although in past times drunkenness and equivocation would have had special topical appeal (see pp. 93–4 below), the wordplay is cumbersome and allusion far-fetched so that, even with a highly skilled performance, attention is likely to drift away, which means that self-confidence also becomes part of what is on display immediately before the murder appears before a full on-stage audience. Macduff obligingly plays along with the performance until his question (l. 39) reveals his own purpose and, perhaps, his and the theatre audience's impatience.

**40–50** The Folio marks Macbeth's entrance before Macduff's question but this position creates an awkward double focus and may be so placed only for the compositor's convenience. An entrance immediately after the question will again seem fatefully timed (see the Commentary at I.ii.25, I.iii.78–88, I.v.28–36, etc.) or, if the actor chooses, may suggest Macbeth had been waiting until he could delay no longer.

With the blood only recently washed from his hands, each one of Macbeth's replies to conventional greetings and enquiries calls for an equivocation that will be hard to achieve and maintain. Macduff's 'joyful trouble' (ll. 45–6) is probably a polite reference to the early hour, but its incomplete verse-line indicates a silence before Macbeth replies and, during this, an audience may *see* that he is afraid of revealing too much of what is in his mind. The brevity of 'This is the door' will call for Macbeth's most assured equivocation, after which Macduff's talk of making 'bold' and the following half-line of silence may be Shakespeare's way of holding attention on him, whether or not he has been entirely successful in masking his inner feelings.

**50–60**   Macbeth finds that replying to Lennox involves even more difficult dissimulation, the qualification of 'he did appoint so' (l. 50) being a sign of fear or, at least, awkwardness. The broken rhythms, accumulation of detail, and widening scope of Lennox's description can give a vivid impression of a 'young' man's (l. 59) amazement and desire to understand and report adequately. In contrast, Macbeth's brief and strangely dismissive reply can scarcely fail to make an audience aware of the very different response that he must conceal. Again the actor will have to judge how much is revealed at this stage of the play.

The dynamics of the dialogue suggest that physically the two performances are as contrasted as their speech: Macbeth probably stands still while Lennox moves around using much of the space afforded by the stage, but the very opposite of this could make a startling effect. Again, a decision has to be made about how much of the hidden truth is shown in performance and here the judgement is one that both actors have to find together as the dialogue proceeds.

**60–77**   The repetition of 'horror' immediately upon entry calls for great vocal power and strong imaginative involvement in what Macduff has seen, a task made more difficult because this is the first major demand made upon the actor. Again repetition is threefold, which may suggest that what is happening is more than normally inevitable. With his second line, Macduff has words more under control, and probably his physical response as well. In reply to brief, perhaps stumbling questions, his involvement grows more sustained and varied. At first, in an exposition that is, in the circumstances, strangely and wilfully extended, he speaks of the dead king as a defaced representative of God. (*Temple* is used here in the biblical sense of a place, or body, in which God Himself resides.) His sense of outrage is now stronger than his terror. To more uncomprehending questions, Macduff starts to give orders, at first turning from religious to mythological reference to express the danger, as well as the horror, of what he has seen.

When the others have left the stage, Macduff continues to give orders and with them further metaphysical, religious, superstitious and supernatural issues are brought into his evocation of the horrendous happening. The ringing of a bell marks its public and ongoing nature. In effect, the drama now fills a greater space than the stage and theatre: it is occurring in the context of the world, history and whatever can be comprehended of eternity.

Some editors have thought that the second textual reference to a bell (l. 77) is a compositor's misreading of a stage direction, but a delayed response to the first command is suitable for a household awoken unexpectedly from sleep. A repeated order will heighten the urgency of the speech when its concluding command might otherwise become too slow and cumbersome.

**78–87**    The half-line of verse indicates that Lady Macbeth enters after Macduff has left the bell to speak for him. She starts as if ignorant of the 'business' but then takes command of the situation, using 'trumpet' and 'parley' to suggest the demands and dangers of open warfare. After Banquo has entered, she conforms more to Macduff's notion of a 'gentle lady' (l. 80): the domesticity of 'what in our house' may overplay an attempt to change the tone of her response. By now Macduff has ignored her and, after greeting Banquo eagerly, makes common cause with him by recounting what has happened in stark terms. The personal tone of 'Dear Duff' suggests that, after briefly responding to the mistress of the house, the two men have moved closer together. They are then silenced by the return of Macbeth and Lennox.

Ross will have nothing to say in this scene and, since he did not go with the other two to Duncan's chamber, he must enter from another direction. Some editors delete the entrance, others explain that he is needed to superintend Lady Macbeth's exit at line 122. However, in the course of the tragedy, Ross is repeatedly the witness to events, at first because he takes orders but increasingly taking initiative himself (see II.iv) and speaking for himself (see V.vi.78–86).

At some time, those named in the stage direction will be joined by others who have been roused by Macduff's alarm: they have dressed rapidly or are not fully dressed, and hold themselves ready for an unknown emergency. The military term 'parley' (l. 79) could imply that some are armed and ready to fight. The stage will be as full as the entire cast can make it and the on-stage action disordered, tense, and probably hushed.

**88–93**   Surprisingly, in contrast to the appalled and short-phrased
utterances of everyone else, Macbeth speaks a sentence of five and a
half verse-lines. And it is not about what he has seen but, mostly,
about the consequences of the murder with regard to his own view of
time and mortality. Unless he speaks aside (which would be difficult
for others on stage), the actor will have to decide whether these
words are a means of covering every other thought (such as the
dangers to himself, his still-burning ambition, or the need for equivocation) or an instinctive (and dangerous) expression of a sense of
guilt or loss. It may be possible for both these reactions to be present.
However the speech is played, the ordering of its words requires well
controlled breathing and an assured physical presence. The half-line
with which he concludes indicates that everyone present is left
speechless.

Echoes are here of Macbeth's soliloquy at the start of Act I, scene v
(see Commentary), in which Duncan arouses thoughts of enduring
virtues and feelings of pity. Both speeches anticipate his later awareness of the 'honour, love, obedience, troops of friends' that he has
lost (V.iii.22–8).

**94–121**   In reply to the younger son of the man he has murdered,
Macbeth's speech pattern changes, seeming both hesitant and firm.
Macduff's more direct response silences him and, as before (ll. 21–8),
'young' Lennox supplies vivid details. Macbeth seizes this as a cue for
confessing, very briefly as if still stunned, two additional murders.
When questioned (Macduff once more taking the lead) Macbeth
changes yet again, first to questions and reasoning and then to a vivid
depiction of what he has just seen, the result of the crime he has
committed. Metaphor and paradox lead to wide-ranging reflection
and then back again to a depiction of what he has done. This time, as
he confesses to murdering the two grooms whom his wife has
smeared with blood, he speaks of love in simple and repetitive
monosyllables, and of a courage that would make it known. At this
moment, his wife calls for help, breaking the tense silence in which
he has been heard and diverting attention.

The actor will have to choose whether Lady Macbeth intervenes,
and subsequently pretends to faint, in order to prevent her husband

saying more and betraying his guilt, or whether she truly faints, unable to bear the tension – a reaction that will occur more disastrously in her last sleepwalking scene (V.i). This decision will depend on the degree of confidence and emotional involvement that Macbeth has shown and how he has borne the physical pressures. Perhaps the best course is to leave the audience in doubt on this score and therefore more unsure than before about how far Macbeth is succeeding in handling the situation. Certainly she unsettles the grouping of others on stage, giving Malcolm and Donalbain an opportunity to move aside and consult together.

**122 to the end**  Banquo's repetition of Macduff's 'Look to the Lady' from six lines earlier and the brief presentation of Duncan's two sons have suggested that the Folio text is deficient here. But the dialogue can serve the dramatic moment well, these very features suiting both the urgency and confusion of the moment. During the young princes' first exchange, others on stage can be occupied with attending to Lady Macbeth, whose fainting calls for investigation before she is carried out; during their second exchange, everyone else can leave the stage and then, on an empty stage, it will gain the audience's total attention for significant narrative details. This handling of the drama is in keeping with the swift progress of the plot and leaves the audience wanting to know more – a state of mind that will be to some extent satisfied and developed by the change of focus and presentation in the next scene.

As it stands, the Folio text may be judged consummate rather than botched or imperfect. Banquo's part in it makes good theatrical sense. He speaks out among those attending to Lady Macbeth without adding to what is already known, but then moves the story forward and widens the perspective. After speaking for others, he closes by establishing his own position: first, a trust in God that no one else has affirmed and then committal to resolute and searching action. Macduff, who until now has taken the lead, agrees at once, followed by everyone else. Macbeth, who has been silent since his wife took attention away from him, resumes control by falling in with the others: in this way he escapes further investigation at this time.

The mixture of proverbial sayings and rapid decisions in the last exchanges of the scene is stylistically strange. In performance, however, it gives to two young actors the means of expressing both their inexperience and awareness of danger. Conspicuously missing is any personal feeling for their murdered father or for each other: whether this was Shakespeare's intention and how it can be used in performance are very open questions for actors and readers.

## Act II, scene iv

**1–20**  As Duncan's sons leave in fear of their lives, an anonymous 'Old Man' enters talking of the past as well as a troubled present. He has not been seen before but Ross is here too, no longer obeying Duncan's orders as in Act I, scene iii, or silent as in Act I, scene vi, and, according to the Folio, as he was in the previous scene. Unhurriedly they speak of a 'sore night' and troubled 'heavens' but referring to recent events only in general terms. Because they avoid the particulars that are fresh in the audience's mind, they may seem to be speaking under duress and in fear of being overheard.

Ross's 'good father' (l. 4) may be a usual courtesy towards an old and trusted acquaintance but, taken together with its repetition immediately before he leaves (l. 39) and the blessing he then receives, it could be intended to show at the start of the scene that the Old Man is a priest. If so, the scene could be played as if in a chapel or hermitage; in early performances the two could be 'discovered' already talking by opening curtains that conceal a small central area to the rear of the stage. The alternative of entering in the middle of a conversation taking place in an unspecified location is awkward with the text as printed – at least it is so in many present-day productions – and may be intended to seem so.

The text stays close to Holinshed's account of the portents that followed Donwald's murder of King Duff (see p. 102) but Ross adds to its judgemental and supernatural implications by introducing a 'bloody' theatrical simile that is a reminder of Macbeth's conscious decision to act (see I.vii.79–82). In the Old Man's reference to the unnatural 'deed that's done' (ll. 10–1), readers (and possibly some audience members) may catch an uncanny echo of Macbeth's 'If 'twere done when 'tis done' at the start of Act I, scene v – a crucial soliloquy in any performance – and his 'I have done the deed' as he returns after the murder (II.ii.15).

**20 to the end**   Macduff does not acknowledge the Old Man's presence so either Ross leads him aside or he keeps his distance as if not trusting a third person with his opinion of the news he brings. Either way of staging will add to a sense of danger in their covert exchange. The attention given to Macduff, which began in the previous scene, is further developed here by showing him to be in possession of important facts, and decisive in following his own political and moral judgement. Both men see beyond the present and much of their exchange is terse, as if under pressure of time or needing maximum secrecy. The incomplete verse-line (l. 33) probably indicates a pause before Macduff reveals where the body has been taken. (The removal is significant: Holinshed tells how it was thought a murdered corpse would bleed in the presence of its killer (see p. 101 below), a superstition Shakespeare had staged in the earlier *Richard III*, I.ii.55–61.)

Even if it is not a priest who gives the blessing that concludes this scene, the short line 39 indicates a pause in which Ross makes some pious or ritualistic preparation for receiving it before he goes off, having made no response to Macduff's parting disclosure of intention, loyalty and foreboding.

# ACT III

## Act III, scene i

**1–10**   For the first time, Banquo is alone on stage. Perhaps he is dressed for a journey, since Macbeth seems to know he will be leaving, but he would have other ways of learning that about a man whom he fears.

The four monosyllables at the start of this soliloquy, followed by the threefold citing of the Witches' prophecy, would suit an energetic entrance, Banquo perhaps having sought and found a private place.

Almost at once his suspicion of his fellow captain becomes evident (and, possibly, his fear of him), and then his 'hope' for his own future. No sooner has the audience heard this than Macbeth enters, crowned and accompanied with fanfares and attendants, the prophecy having been fulfilled. The narrative has taken a great step forward.

**11–39**   Alerted to Banquo's thoughts as the stage fills with a ceremonial display of Macbeth's new status, the audience will know very well what lies unspoken behind the king's talk with his potential rival. Perhaps he plays with the situation's ironies by addressing the opening remark to his wife, for she immediately takes up his theme, adding to the ironies. The half-line (l. 86) may indicate that at this point Banquo pays formal homage.

Although the audience does not know it, Macbeth has already sought out assassins to deal with Banquo and is likely to sharpen his enquiries so that he can give them accurate and sufficient instructions. Three half-lines of verse indicate pauses in what could otherwise be a casual exchange of information: Macbeth is acting geniality and friendship, Banquo hiding his suspicions. After giving information about Duncan's sons, perhaps as a sign of trust, Macbeth's further question about Banquo's son is of crucial importance to them both: to hide this he speaks with the casual air of last-minute thoughtfulness. Banquo will have to acknowledge the enquiry as a mark of friendship and courtesy but his words are few and betray little; he says nothing on his exit, again alerting the audience to his unspoken thoughts.

**40–7**   With the air of a considerate and easy host, Macbeth ensures his own privacy. Several incomplete verse-lines allow time for his message to be received and for the stage to empty. Everyone will wait for Lady Macbeth to leave first, taking precedence and receiving expressions of respect as the newly crowned Queen: this will take some time to effect so the audience will have a good view of her.

Once alone, Macbeth acts swiftly, surprising the audience, who did not know he had already taken initiatives. Once the servant has left, he speaks of his concern in the briefest terms, with 'thus' and 'nothing' in place of the earlier 'fair' and 'foul' that he and the Witches have both used (I.i.9 and I.iii.37). If this echo is marked in any way, Macbeth's progress can seem either fated or motivated by an insecurity that lies deep within his mind. The audience may not recognize this but the actor will.

**48–71**  Words and sentences are simple at first as Macbeth sets out the situation, his fears now briefly named but contrasted with Banquo's 'royalty ... dauntless temper ... wisdom'. Then, as he recalls the Witches' prophecies, syntax gains a longer reach and soon the horror and pain of insecurity fill his mind and are expressed with the active physical imagery of 'grip ... wrenched ... filed ... murdered ... rancours'. These are the sensations that 'stick deep' (l. 49) and, again, phrases tighten, with repetitions and exclamations, as he challenges 'fate' itself, as if in a tournament to be fought to the death – a pre-vision of the tragedy's conclusion, foreshortened into few words and omitting its demand for fortitude and pain. The 'gracious Duncan' still haunts his mind; his immortal soul is still a 'jewel'. However clearly and soberly the actor sets out the situation, changes of imagery, rhythm and syntax finally bring the speech to an active and upbeat conclusion. How confident that is depends on the actor's performance: how much weight is given to the concluding words; how settled are Macbeth's posture and sensations: how far fear and insecurity have been banished from his mind.

**72–117**  Although the play-text is short, for performances today, lines are often cut from Macbeth's meeting with the two Murderers. Few directors find any purpose to be served by the full text or any reason for making an audience pay the necessary attention to follow all its complicated exposition and devious interchanges. Yet while editors debate Shakespeare's authorship in other scenes (see p. 8 above), here they usually take it for granted. One positive advantage of the full text is that it demonstrates how convoluted is Macbeth's mind as he plans Banquo's death. Another is the establishing of two lawless and dispirited persons as representatives of an unsettled and dangerous Scotland.

From all three actors the dialogue calls for concentrated listening and varying contact with each other, otherwise they will lose the audience's attention. These three have spoken previously on the same subject but now Macbeth is about to tell them that Banquo must be killed. He speaks of his 'enemy' in very different terms from those of the preceding soliloquy, which may lead the audience to think that all he says now is a fabrication. And perhaps the Murderers' assent is a pretence, their two replies (ll. 107–13) coming so readily and so assertively, before they know what they are being asked to do. Played along these lines, their talk can have a dangerous edge as each side deceives the other. There will also be an overarching need for absolute secrecy.

Talk of 'half a soul' and 'a notion crazed', followed by a catalogue of dogs and men, allows a dark, sardonic humour to surface but the digression can also be evidence of a 'deep' reluctance to come to the 'point' of their second meeting (ll. 82 and 85) – which, long before it is spoken of, is the assassination of Banquo. From its start, this private encounter is difficult to act, for the actors and for the persons in the play, and that was probably Shakespeare's intention because the suggestion of unspoken restraints and pressures beneath the words takes the play's action into new, clandestine territory in which the hero will seem belittled and his concerns trivialized.

Nevertheless, on 'bounteous nature' and 'grapple' (ll. 97 and 105), Macbeth comes close to expressing his own deep sense of what can be lost and the effort needed to follow the course he has set himself. He will hear the fluent responses of the murderers eagerly, making no comment but moving on to the nub of their business. As he sees the prospect of safety, he speaks of blood and his need for immediate action.

**117 to the end**    Although still troubled with thoughts of friendship and guilt (ll. 120–3), Macbeth presses forward, paying little attention to what the willing Murderers are saying. He shows a command of detail and, in speaking of Banquo's son, talks of 'embrac[ing] the fate / Of that dark hour' as if he were, for the moment, at ease with his own murderous thoughts. He hurries his two accomplices away (l. 139), but not too far because he depends upon them. They say nothing more and may well be confused and need the reassurance of line 139. Once they are gone, the concluding couplet ensures a rare moment when Macbeth is fully and even buoyantly committed to murder – perhaps because, this time, he will not 'do the deed' himself.

## Act III, scene ii

**1–12**     The short exchange with the servant can sound entirely casual and, certainly, this would be the intended effect. Then, with a sudden change, once she is alone, Lady Macbeth's 'words' are powered by the same insecurity as her husband's at the start of his last soliloquy (III.ii 47–8), only they are more succinct and apparently untroubled by thoughts of anyone but themselves. The soliloquy moves lightly at first, which is perhaps an expression of the fear that, immediately afterwards, is emphasized in a further alliterative couplet (ll. 6–7).

Once her husband is present, and before he can say a word, Lady Macbeth is fully in command of herself and takes charge of him. She knows very well that he is 'afraid to think what [he has] done' (II.ii. 51) but insists, 'What's done is done.'

**13–28**     As if struggling with the serpent in his mind, Macbeth does not argue but, after an irregular and incomplete first line, he continues to counter-state what his wife has said, with scarcely another pause but a still sharper physical image. That done he takes on heaven and hell and the more immediate shaking of his own nightly and terrible dreams, and the threat of insanity – his 'restless ecstasy'. Thinking of Duncan at peace after death, he falls silent, a state of mind from which his wife has to rouse him with the immediate necessities of concealment and pretence. With the one line 28, Macbeth seems to obey freely, speaking now to his 'love'. For the moment they are at peace and here actors will often embrace; even a touch will seem to offer hope of escape from what is destroying all 'content' (l. 5).

**29–39**     Macbeth instructs his wife as she has taught him (see I.v.60–70 and II.ii.71–2) but his insecurity remains and, after a half-line pause, 'Unsafe the while . . .' betrays something of this. She sees more in his bearing and face than he acknowledges, as her brief reproof shows. They may have separated by this time but, when her intervention releases a fuller confession of his tormented mind, he broaches the subject of Banquo's descendants. A measure of the renewed trust and intimacy between them is the 'dear wife' by which he addresses her. Probably they are looking closely into each other's eyes when she answers by alluding to the possibility of murder, because he then does so more directly (ll. 38–9).

**40 to the end**    'Jocund' is a light-hearted, cheerful word that brings a surprising change of mood that progressively creates a barrier between them. In his imagination he becomes sensitive to the small, almost noiseless sounds of the hours of darkness and is aware of a dangerous, non-human command. 'What's to be done?' shows that he has taken the initiative, and the exceptional 'dearest chuck' marks a further change in their relationship: he is silent about his commit- tal to a 'dreadful' action but familiar towards his wife, intimate and affectionate as if compensating for a new distance between them. Then, addressing the night, he cuts off from her entirely, his mind full of what his action will involve.

The blending of sensitivity and resolve, pain and loneliness, shows his imagination at full stretch and leaves his wife speechless. When, once more, he is aware of her presence, he assumes command in a concluding couplet that also acknowledges the 'ill' he is about to do. The half-line that, unusually, follows the final rhymed couplet indi- cates a silence before she leaves with him. The *exeunt* that follows will focus attention closely on the two actors as the crisis in their rela- tionship is resolved one way or another. They can leave closely together or with contrasting steps and some distance apart; he could take her arm, or she his. Almost certainly an audience will want to know more and will be left waiting for the outcome.

### Act III, scene iii

**1–14**    The entrance of *three* Murderers shifts attention surprisingly. Action is about to take over from speech and the unexpected pres- ence of a third provides an echo of the earlier arrival of three Witches.

With the one word, 'Macbeth', the audience is left to guess that the third has been sent to 'leave no rubs or botches in the work' (III.i.133) and so keep insecurity at bay. There is no argument but the First Murderer's next speech shows that tension has relaxed.

While it establishes the time and place, the reflective account of twilight and a 'timely inn' is out of key with everything else the Murderers have said. A present-day actor trying to motivate the sudden transition would be helped if a long silence preceded these words, giving time for reflection and establishing a need to say something. But given the basic tensions of the situation, a heightened and exceptional awareness needs no conscious justification.

**8 to the end**   A sound from off-stage alerts actors and audience and then lines 12–24 explain how the ambush has been planned. Fleance's torch still further establishes that it is night time, and Banquo's talk of rain suggests an ease of mind that is immediately displaced by the Murderer's mocking response (l. 16) and recourse to action. Banquo struggles sufficiently to need all three assailants to kill him, with many sword strokes, as it is later reported (see III.iv.25–7). However, he keeps sufficiently clear-headed to order Fleance to escape, rather than stay and try to save his father's life: this shows either prudence or a fated working out of the Witches' prophecy – perhaps both. With the few words that are essential for the audience's understanding of what has happened, the scene is soon over but only after a half-line's pause in which their failure to deal with Fleance can register in the minds of an audience.

### Act III, scene iv

**1–13**   The Folio's brief stage direction, '*Banquet prepared*', may well imply the same elaborate stage business that preceded the off-stage entertainment of Duncan at the start of Act I, scene vii. Certainly this is intended to be a 'great feast' and 'solemn supper' (III.i.12, and 14), or, perhaps, a smaller gathering before that main celebration, a sense of *banquet* common in Shakespeare's plays. Certainly, two 'states' [*raised and/or canopied thrones*] are placed at the head of a large table or tables.

All the actors that the company can supply will crowd onto the stage, marking a major new event after a sequence of scenes that, for the most part, involved very few persons.

The opening dialogue suggests considerable formality, which is mitigated by the hosts' courteous words of welcome. Macbeth's 'Play . . . humble . . . require' are words, however, that can carry private ironies. While mingling with his guests he does not notice the Murderer's entry, or pretends he does not. Either way, the audience is likely to become aware of his presence before it is acknowledged. The 'blood upon [his] face' may be noticeable at once but that would indicate an unlikely haste or carelessness: alternatively, its presence could be entirely in Macbeth's guilty imagination and another sign of his haunted conscience.

**14–31**   Throughout this meeting the two men must speak secretly and aside but Macbeth has a heightened awareness – either a new confidence expressed at first in callow wordplay or a residual fear held at bay by the same means. A half-line silence follows the news of Fleance's escape and then a 'fit' of fear or guilt again threatens to take possession of his mind. As at other times, the thought of what he has done starts Macbeth thinking of what he has lost (see Commentary, I.vii.1–27 and III.i.48–71, etc.) and dialogue shifts towards soliloquy: here he becomes aware of his need of freedom and a secure standing (ll. 20–2). About other matters, his talk is short-phrased and almost abrupt. When he thinks of the future, he dismisses the Murderer to rejoin the others on stage, who, meanwhile, will have been more or less silently engaged in the banquet and giving, perhaps, a show of good spirits.

**31–51**   Still sitting in her 'state', Lady Macbeth takes the lead with a reasonably expressed reproof, laced with proverbial wisdom. He says nothing at first, as if still lost in his own thoughts, and delays joining his guests until both Lennox and Ross have made very much the same request. Lennox is a young thane trying to cover up the present awkwardness but Ross, the audience knows, has sought help in coping with the 'unnatural' aftermath of Duncan's death and so his words will be more carefully chosen (II.iv.1–20).

A trapdoor, lighting effects and projected images have all been used to bring Banquo's ghost on stage but, with strong and well differentiated performances, the audience's attention may be deflected from the moment of entrance naturally enough. Dr Forman's account of a performance in 1611 tells how the ghost entered behind Macbeth (see, p. 4 above). Once on stage (the Folio marks this immediately before Macbeth's 'Sweet remembrancer!') the ghost is likely to draw many eyes and the audience to sense the recognition that is coming before it occurs, and, being prepared, may tend to share in it. When the audience members realize that no one else on stage sees what Macbeth and each of them can plainly see, they are likely to become keenly aware of his isolation.

He speaks with matter-of-fact directness at first (ll. 46–50), partly because he will half-expect such a sight but more because he knows he must keep control of himself. Incomplete verse-lines, however, suggest two major silences and, after the second (l. 50), some kind of physical breakdown prevents him saying more and leaves his wife to take complete control of him and everyone else.

**52–73** Either Macbeth has moved away from the table, appalled by what he has seen, or his wife has drawn him apart. Briefly she has to explain what has happened and urge their guests to maintain normal behaviour before she gains sufficient privacy to speak her mind to her husband. She does this with a compact force – 'Are you a man?' (l. 57) – using words that echo those with which she had held him to his purpose immediately before the killing of Duncan (see I.vii.46–51). His first reply is assertively short-phrased and simple (ll. 59–60), which only causes her to continue by denying what he sees and caustically mocking his weakness.

When he realizes she cannot see the ghost he answers by pointing in its direction and then addressing the gory ghost directly, who, alarmingly, answers with silent nods. The audience will be acutely aware that the second murder, by which Macbeth had hoped to gain security and defeat his rival's hope of the succession for his heirs, could at any moment be revealed to everyone present. At this point, the ghost leaves as if its task was done. No trick is needed here; it can simply walk from the stage between the guests and servants as they are seated once more at the banquet or busy about it.

All Macbeth does is to turn to his wife and say what he saw (l. 73), as if asking for belief, either because he fears he is going mad or because he needs her belief, her help, or, more basically, her company. He has regained some control but the divided halves of line 73 show two people diametrically opposed in response to what has happened: for one it is very real, for the other a shameful folly. As this banquet scene develops, the two principal actors have to pace their performances so that they grow by degrees towards its double and very different climaxes of terror and assertion of their wills. Gradually, a great gulf is exposed between them; they will become barely able to communicate with each other.

**74–91**   Other actors on stage will find difficulty in remaining credibly present but out of focus during the time the two principals hold attention, particularly after the ghost has left. Yet they are a continuous reminder of Macbeth's isolation and of the kingdom he has won and is now in danger of losing. Perhaps their presence cues him to speak of the 'olden time' and 'gentle weal' [*peaceful society*], but on earlier occasions his thoughts have seemed to lead back naturally to what has been lost; this time it is with no lessening of the present horror, 'too terrible for the ear'.

When his wife reminds him to rejoin his guests, calling them noble and himself her 'worthy lord', and perhaps leading the way back, he is ready to do so. At first he avoids naming Banquo and may put on a 'fairest show' (I.vii.81) by speaking with a degree of belief in the possibility of a 'general joy' (l. 88). Or he may have become so helpless that he can do no more than what she asks. For a short time everyone joins in and good order begins to be restored, at least outwardly. Tensions relax until Macbeth dares to name Banquo and prepares to drink his health: at which point the ghost returns and, with it, Macbeth's fit.

**92–107**   The change in Macbeth is immediate. An old theatre tradition has him throw the cup of wine at the ghost, who continues to 'glare' at him. While reaction among others will be widespread, a mixture of incredulity and terror, he ignores them all as he tries to exorcise what is totally real to him and inexorably holds his fascinated attention. At the first opportunity, Lady Macbeth turns to the thanes, the phrasing of her words less confident than before, her argument at first unlikely and then merely obvious.

'What man dare . . .' (l. 98) could be addressed to himself or the ghost, or to his wife in answer to her taunt, 'Are you a man?' (l. 57). As a short first-line it stands alone, with a terrible silence before or after. When he does dare to face the ghost, he summons far-fetched yet palpable images of ferocity and danger in a sustained outpouring of words that marks the climax of this second encounter. Emotionally, intellectually and physically, he is exerting the utmost of all that he possesses. In his imagination he is fighting for his life even as he contemplates defeat. Then, suddenly, he finds himself alone (as happens in a dream) and with simple words, as if nothing has happened, he turns to his guests. Probably this is so strange that Lady Macbeth feels bound to tell him the effect of what he has experienced only a moment before.

If Banquo's ghost nods its head towards Macbeth as it is leaving – he did this on his previous exit – the act of his going will be a declaration that a fight to the death will, indeed, be required of his murderer.

**108–20** Macbeth may now be near exhaustion and lying on the floor or slumped over the table. With little pressure behind his words, he could be speaking only to his wife or, equally suitably, to everyone present, or to himself as he searches the faces of those who surround him. And yet, despite the very obvious change of mood and passion, his wife says later that he has grown worse and urges everyone to leave, which they do at once and without further questions. It may well be that, instead of giving way to exhaustion, he is still standing, his frustration informing this very different speculation. Or perhaps, as with a great unstoppable animal, his instinctive will exercises control over his wounded spirits and fatigued body.

On the page, the lords and attendants leave the banquet very quickly, but in performance, some considerable time will be taken as each individual finds his way out and cups and flagons and other stage properties are given even minimal attention. If there is no 'order' in their going, as they have been told, they will bunch together at the doors and delay matters further. All this will have a very different feel from the start of the scene and a hiatus almost certainly occurs when the king and queen are left alone to sit down, together or apart. By the time they do speak, the audience will be ready to pay the closest attention.

**121 to the end**    The belief that a murdered man's blood will betray the most secret murderer and cause his death was a superstition found in many histories and folktales (see commentary at the end of II.iv). Macbeth is speaking of the worst of fates and, at the same time, thinking of what he might do and who might be his enemy. He does not communicate fully with his wife, who now, in notable contrast to only moments before, takes no initiative. 'What is the night?' may be the start of active planning and his next question confirms this. The information that he keeps spies in every household, and the time needed to establish this, are signs that either his insecurity or his ambition has been a long-standing concern in his mind, but his thoughts are now on the future.

Without saying when he reached the conclusion – the repetitive phrasing suggests that it may be at this very moment – he senses that the Witches are essential to his security, in their function as 'Weird Sisters' or, in Holinshed's words, 'the goddesses of destiny' or some 'nymphs or fairies endued with knowledge of prophecy'. Meeting them again, Macbeth will credit them with yet broader powers (see IV.i.49–59) but now he acknowledges that they are the 'worst means' that he can use. An image of wading into a river or sea of blood looks back to line 121, with the added thoughts of weariness and precipitate action.

Perhaps remembering or, possibly, forgetting the voice that had cried 'Sleep no more' (II.ii.34), Lady Macbeth tells him that he has to sleep if he is to live and thrive. He agrees to go, but hopes for no easy release from his predicament. After the customary couplet on *Exeunt*, a further short line may be intended as encouragement to Lady Macbeth or a harsh joke at his own inability to do more; possibly it is both. Or it could be a brave defiance of fate and physical weakness. Which of these it is will depend on how the entire scene has been played.

Another element that will be improvised or finely tuned in performance is the readiness with which she follows him. A very strong Lady Macbeth could leave before him, her previous short speeches being scornful reproofs without trace of sympathy; his dependence would then be very obvious.

## Act III, scene v

**Entry stage direction**    The authorship of the whole of this scene and Hecat's appearance in Act IV, scene i, has often been ascribed to someone other than Shakespeare. The style of writing differs from elsewhere in the play, including the other Witches' scenes. Thomas Middleton has been named as their author because, as noted above (pp. 6–8), the songs at the end of this scene and at IV.i.43 are found in full in his play *The Witch*, where they fit their context far better than here.

Accepting the Folio text of *Macbeth* as the King's Men play ascribed to Shakespeare, the song and some dialogue from *The Witch* are quoted here (modernized and regularized) as keys to the effect Hecat might be expected to make in performance, especially if played in a venue that had machinery for flying:

HECATE    Hie thee home with 'em:
    Look well to the house tonight: I am for aloft.
FIRESTONE    Aloft, quoth you? I would you would break your neck once,
    that I might have all quickly. Hark, hark Mother! They are above the
    steeple already, flying over your head with a noise [*sound*] of musicians.
HECATE    They are [*there*] indeed: help, help me! I'm too late else.
SONG (*in the air*)    *Come away! Come away!*
                    *Hecate, Hecate, come away!*
HECATE [*singing*]    *I come, I come, I come, I come,*
                   *With all the speed I may,*
                   *With all the speed I may.*
    Where's Stadlin?
[A VOICE] (*in the air*)    Here!
HECATE (*going up*)    *Now I go, now I fly,*
                *Malkin, my sweet spirit, and I,*
            *Oh what a dainty pleasure 'tis*
               *To ride in the air*
               *When the moon shines fair*
            *And sing and dance, and toy and kiss.*

The differences from the Folio text in verbal style and content are obvious, but the simple elaboration and repetitions of the song indicate a performance style that would change the nature of an audience's attention, and suggest that another mechanism operates in the play's action, one that is strangely inhuman and tantalizingly uninformative. However, the speech for Hecat in the Folio differs from this model in metre, rhythm, syntax, vocabulary, imagery, allusion and structure: it is far more authoritative and more demanding on the actor and audience. Shakespeare's Hecat is a goddess and Middleton's only a chief witch among others.

The stage direction for '*Thunder*' repeats those in earlier Witches' scenes but a new element is '*meeting*', which implies that, even if Hecat does not enter by flying or on an upper level of the stage, the goddess should enter from a direction opposite to that used by her subjects, as if she belongs to another locale or other world.

**1–13**    At a glance the audience should be able to see in Hecat's silent presence what has caused the First Witch's opening words. She should be so impressive that if the Witches use the same strange gestures, dance-steps, and mixture of independent and unified responses of their earlier scenes, they will all three prostrate themselves in front of this superior being, even before she speaks. The entry direction suggests that they approach Hecat, and not the other way around: they could act as if under orders that are received unwillingly, cowering together in apprehension and fear or making ritual signs of submission.

When Hecat speaks of her own powers (ll. 6–7), the Witches, who are her agents and worshippers, will make ingratiating signs of acquiescence, which might change to expressions of pride and relief when she speaks of '*our* art' (l. 9) and so makes common cause with them. Lines 10 to 13 apply more particularly to Macbeth and, being 'worse', will be sharper in reproof: on hearing this, the three Witches might scatter to opposite and extreme corners of the stage, to be left trembling in still greater fear of punishment for wrong-doing. And with the reference to Macbeth, the audience will better understand the matter in hand.

**14–33**    When Hecat offers her hearers hope (see l. 14), they will completely change their response, showing relief and an eagerness to obey, held back only by a need to listen intently to instructions. On talk of their 'vessels . . . spells . . . charms and everything beside', they will know what to do and confidence will be restored only to be mixed with awe when Hecat speaks of the fateful part that she will play in their work.

With 'Great business' (l. 22), Hecat starts to give details of her plan and tells a story that will hold attention on stage and among the theatre audience. With the minute detail of a 'vaporous drop' and reference to a distance far beyond any human's reach, she may well be heard in absolute silence and stillness. As she reaches the climax with promise of Macbeth's 'confusion' [destruction, ruin], the Witches' close attention can change to vocal and physical expressions of satisfaction, the text's metre, rhythm and rhymes supporting a major response to this conclusion. Hecat probably waits for silence and stillness before continuing and, in a new rhythm, making a further prophecy that is contained within a couplet (ll. 30–1); this foretells the effect of what will happen and is not restricted to events as the earlier prophecies have been.

As the short lines 32 and 33 establish yet another rhythm, they give an explanation of all that will follow. Brief and gnomic, this speech encapsulates and emphasizes one of the main themes of the play that Macbeth has already enunciated (III.iv.20–4) and that the play's action will repeatedly exemplify (see IV.i.81–3).

**34 to the end**    A double direction for singing, further changes of rhythm, and no indication of Hecat's exit in the Folio text (which the Penguin edition closely follows), are further signs that an earlier text has been adapted to fit in here. The First Witch's concluding line suggests that, once the singing starts, she and her fellows have been awestruck, able to do little more than show their respect and pay attention to their mistress and 'contriver of all harms' (ll. 6–7); but now, with their 'haste', the scene closes rapidly.

## Act III, scene vi

**1–23**    No indication is given of where this scene takes place, except that it must be out of earshot from everyone else. This talk is dangerous and, at line 21, Lennox insists on silence or lower voices. As noted already (p. 7 above), this scene was almost certainly written to follow Act IV, scene i, and was moved to its present position when the Hecat scene (III.v) was added. As it stands here, the information given is impossibly up-to-date; the anonymous Lord already knows that Macduff has rebuffed Macbeth's messenger and is now fled to England (ll. 29ff.) although the latter fact is reported as if for the first time at IV.i.141–2.

With his first words, Lennox implies that they are continuing a conversation that was not entirely clear because, it may be assumed, of the need for secrecy. The irony that Lennox uses is so heavy that it is easy to see through it to the disaster that he knows has occurred. If laboured in performance the double meanings can become absurd and so some actors take the speech lightly, with Lennox pretending to be ignorant of any serious implications. It should, however, become progressively clear that he is testing this Lord's loyalties as he, also, is being watched carefully for similar reasons. Finally, by plainly calling Macbeth a 'tyrant', Lennox becomes more open and shares the news he has received about Macduff, asking for more news in return. Trust has been established and the Lord responds by giving his news of Malcolm.

Before this scene, Lennox has been a young thane who is quick to respond and ask questions; now he is careful and more subtle, and will soon become forthright.

**24–45**    Like the Old Man at the end of Act II, the Lord introduces a wider and more obviously Christian dimension to the play. He immediately picks up and adopts Lennox's use of *tyrant* and, without pause, passes on to speak of 'the most pious Edward' and his ability to bring redress. That opens up the prospect of war and, similarly, Macduff's rebuff of Macbeth's messenger is news that makes personal vendetta probable. Lennox registers the growing danger.

The Lord's reference to 'Him above' (ll. 32–3) introduces a vision of a nation enjoying peace and plenty, couched in terms that reflect what had been intended by the royal banquet of two scenes previously and which it conspicuously failed to deliver.

**45 to the end** Having no more questions, Lennox now introduces a more formal prayer. Both actors will have relaxed their performances as mutual trust has been won, and now a shared ritual gesture could unite them further. They might kneel together but then, as they leave the stage, thunder shatters the calm for the beginning of the next Act.

# ACT IV

## Act IV, scene i

**1–38** An insistent presence in the minds of Macbeth and Banquo but seen only with Hecat since the start of Act I, the Witches now take over the stage to the sound of thunder. They are totally involved in their own rituals, which are much as they were before: threefold speaking in turn, obedience to off-stage familiar spirits, and a concern with the right time for what they do. But their appearance takes the play's narrative a great step ahead because the audience knows they are here to meet Hecat, their goddess-mistress, at the mouth of hell – 'the pit of Acheron' (III.v.15) – and that together they will encounter Macbeth a second time and 'draw him on to his confusion' (III.v.15 and 29). The audience also knows that Macbeth has decided to put all other 'causes' aside to meet early in the morning with the 'Weird Sisters' and so learn his fate – to 'know / By the worst means the worst' (III.iv.131–4). Seldom does a new scene have such thorough preparation with expectation so clearly defined and yet, knowing so much, the audience is now kept waiting while the Witches 'wind up' a charm by encircling a cauldron that has appeared on stage, probably through a trapdoor where it will later descend (see l. 105).

Even the simplest staging of this scene will face practical difficulties, all of which were added by Shakespeare to what he had read in the *Chronicles*. Repeatedly it is said that a fire burns and cauldron bubbles, effects that somehow need to be represented on stage. It will always be nigh impossible to provide a recognizable object for each and every ingredient that is 'thrown' into this cauldron. If that were attempted the effect could easily become absurd while creating problems for the actors, who would have to find each ingredient in the correct order. (Very occasionally a production will do just that and emphasize the comic consequences of this and other elements of the Witches' antics, by this means making the accurate prophecies the product of some other agency, a superhuman Fate, as in a Greek tragedy, or the hallucinatory projection of Macbeth's will to power and his incipient guilt.) Later, a series of apparitions must rise and descend from beneath the stage and, finally, eight crowned kings must enter and leave in steady sequence. Everyone involved in this scene – on stage, backstage, and under the stage – has much to do that requires careful forethought. Braced to cope with any eventuality, they will await each performance with a degree of apprehension that may communicate to the audience subliminally.

At the start, the actors alone can provide a strong effect by the combination of an insistent pulse in all they do and say, co-ordinated and rhythmic movement, clear diction, and a total involvement in the mysterious operation in which three successive speeches grow longer and more weighty in their verbal messages. It is possible to differentiate the three Witches, the first ready to take initiatives, the second the most eager to act, the third stronger and more decisive than the others. By establishing these contrasts, the unison of their shared dialogue will stand out from other speeches and suggest a further access of power. A beating drum, music, or strange unearthly sounds can accompany and emphasize the rituals. Something looking like steam should be released to mark the moment when the charm is complete, and accompany the cooling of its ingredients with blood.

**39–43**  Thunder or a reprise of music from her earlier scene might announce Hecat's arrival with three more witches but an equally impressive entry could be managed silently and suddenly, without any preparation (as suggested by the Folio text). She could descend from above the stage (see the Commentary on III.v, entry stage direction), as she is required to leave. As with all show-stopping theatrical spectacles, much depends on how the scene has been handled until this moment.

As noted already, this entry is likely to have been added after the play was first written and both Hecat and the extra witches can be omitted with little loss. Although some reappearance is to be expected after her earlier scene, what she says this time does not have the same verbal and metrical authority as before, likens the Witches to 'elves and fairies' as nowhere else in the play, and achieves almost nothing of significance. Altogether Hecat is now far more reminiscent of Middleton's *The Witch* than on her earlier appearance or in the handling of witches elsewhere in this play. However, when the first Hecat scene is included in a performance, there is little alternative to staging this entry as well, and in a more fully developed form than the Folio requires.

The song quoted in the Folio text appears in *The Witch*, where it is headed: 'A Charm Song: about a vessel'. In a modernized form it reads:

> Black spirits, and white; red spirits, and gray,
> Mingle, mingle, mingle, you that mingle may.
> > Titty, Tiffin: keep it stiff in;
> > Fire-drake, Puckey, make it lucky,
> > Liard, Robin, you must bob in.
> Round, around, around, about, about:
> All ill come running in, all good keep out.

| | |
|---|---|
| 1 WITCH | Here's the blood of a bat. |
| HECATE | Put in that; oh put in that. |
| 2 WITCH | Here's a libard's bane [*leopard's poison*]. |
| HECATE | Put in, again. |
| 1 WITCH | The juice of toad, the oil of adder . . . [etc.] |

This does not fit into Shakespeare's play but suits the tone adopted by Hecat here and elements of it are usable: some adaptation would be necessary.

**44–62** The second Witch's couplet, followed by her command, effectively stops all previous business. Macbeth has been given a strong entry, his first phrase occupying the full length of an iambic line before he briefly interrogates the expectant Witches. With these words, distinct from all others in this scene, he seems in full control and in no way awed by where he is or whom he addresses. Accepting without comment the Witches' mysterious and unified reply (l. 48), he takes a yet more positive step by 'conjuring' them.

Not waiting for agreement, he declares himself ready to face a great range of terrible disasters rather than go without an answer. The single sustained sentence of this remarkable speech builds in rhythmic force as its imaginary vision grows more comprehensively destructive. It will never be easy for the actor to answer all its technical demands without showing the effort: he will have to sustain and harness his breathing if he is to finish without loss of projection or clarity. Brought off without hesitation and almost flawlessly, it will project Macbeth at the peak of his imaginative powers and determination.

The Witches' threefold answer draws him into the net they have prepared, with the theatre audience conscious of what is at stake.

**63–93**   The apparitions are usually staged by means of puppets or manikins that enter through the same trapdoor as the cauldron so that they can be operated from beneath the stage or by one of the Witches. Usually music or other sounds as well as the specified '*Thunder*' help to create an awesome effect to prepare for unusual happenings.

Faced by the first Apparition, Macbeth tries to put a question, as he had demanded he should be able to do, but he stops when told there is no need. For the second, he is ready to listen and say nothing, assuming that his thoughts will be known (see ll. 68–9). When the third arises unbidden, he questions what it is but is again told to say nothing and again he does so. On its disappearance, he is confident of its meaning and is deceived – as he and the audience will discover in time.

Taken together, the Apparitions have the effect of setting a distance between the audience and Macbeth. While he gains in confidence, nothing happens through his initiative: any spectator must surely realize that he is being manipulated. His commanding voice and presence on entry to this scene have gone and he does not seem conscious of the loss. The threefold beat established by the Witches from the start of the tragedy has sounded repeatedly and it must now seem that what Macbeth takes to be 'fair' may yet be 'foul', as they had proclaimed in chorus at the close of the play's very first scene.

The audience is likely to grasp a basic meaning for all the 'sights' (l. 154, below) without the help of words but the implication of the 'bloody babe' is not entirely clear until just before Macbeth's death when Macduff says that he was 'untimely ripped' from his mother's womb (V.vi.54–5). The meaning of the 'armed head' will be more fully appreciated when Macbeth's severed head is brought on stage carried by Macduff, the victor of the last fight. Taken together, the three Apparitions are an epitome of the play's action and a summation of the Witches' prophetic power (see also, pp. 157–8 below).

**94–110** Macbeth now greets his 'worst' (III.iv.134) as 'good' but a question follows and his new confidence, expressed in rhymed couplets, cannot be complete or deep because his heart still 'throbs to know one thing'. He has remembered the fourth prophecy from Act I, scene iii, and therefore demands, on his 'eternal curse', to know if Banquo's issue will ever 'reign in this kingdom'. When he insists on being told, everything changes: the cauldron disappears, music sounds, and the Witches successively agree to 'show' what will 'grieve his heart'. This time, he hears no prophecies but is shown a royal pageant and is left to supply the appropriate words.

**111–23** A procession of kings across the stage seems to be called for by 'line' (l. 116) and this is what is provided in most productions and visual illustrations of the play. But the command 'Down' after Macbeth's first response makes best sense if each 'shadow' (l. 110) has risen, like the other apparitions, from below the stage, this entrance having been made easier by removal of the cauldron. In this reading of the text, 'line' would refer to the *line*-age or succession of Banquo's descendants, in keeping with the use of 'line' later (l. 52); the kings could then be represented by the same kind of puppets or manikins as the earlier apparitions. This procedure would have the advantage of giving the same kind of illusion to all four 'shows'. It would also avoid the heavy casting and costuming demands of the last of them.

However staged, the dumb show will take considerable time to enact. If there is no accompanying music, a number of silences are likely to occur while the eight figures come and go, during which time the audience's attention will revert to Macbeth as his eyeballs are said to 'sear' and his eyes to 'start'. His whole composure will be changing, physically and mentally, as he now calls the Witches 'filthy hags' and as 'his heart' grieves (l. 109). He finishes with a simple exclamation and fearful question that leave him standing 'amazedly' (l. 125).

**124–31**  A changed verbal style and the prominent role that the First Witch assumes (see ll. 128–9) have been taken as signs that this speech was written for Hecat by whoever made the other revisions to the text. Some culmination of the Witches' contribution to the action must surely be required and the presence of Hecat would be a fitting way of providing this. Alternatively, if the earlier music and dances have been striking and capable of strong development, they might be sufficient for this purpose, with or without the First Witch's words, especially if some device enabled the Witches to '*vanish*' as at I.ii.77. In the eighteenth and nineteenth centuries, the exit of a much larger number of witches was greatly elaborated (see below, pp. 117 and 123).

**131–42**  This exchange is puzzling in several ways: news of Macduff has already been given; Lennox has already distanced himself from Macbeth and yet he now reverts to an earlier subservience. 'Come in' and 'came by' suggest a familiar and interior location, nothing like 'the pit of Acheron' (III.v.15) or the open location of the start of this scene. But played strongly enough, the rapid provision of new information and Macbeth's new state of mind have been found sufficient to hold attention and maintain credibility. A degree of uncertainty may be useful preparation for the more sustained speech that follows and introduces key elements in the narrative and presentation of the tragic hero.

**143 to the end**  Although Lennox has to remain on stage (see ll. 154–5), this speech has many marks of a soliloquy in that it moves from self-awareness to general reflection, and then to a decision to act. Except for 'no more sights!' the Witches are forgotten, so that exclamation could be played as a resolve to keep a grasp on reality rather than a fear of returning into their power.

In performance a significant element in this speech is a sense of immediacy and urgency, especially valuable because Macbeth will not return to the stage for almost 400 lines, by far his longest absence. The scene ends briskly, which, for an audience, can have a chilling effect because what he will not stop to think about are 'dread exploits' of gratuitous and merciless violence.

## Act IV, scene ii

**1–30** The appearance on stage of a mother and child takes the narrative forward in a new direction, even before the first words are spoken. For all his later bravery, this son is clearly much younger than Fleance, Banquo's son (see ll. 59–60, 64, and 83–4). Speech starts with a question that is left unanswered but the audience will not take long to grasp its implication and, in doing so, be drawn into Lady Macduff's distress and anxiety.

The presence of Ross is significant in the wider issues of the play. First acting as Duncan's envoy and then remaining silent after the king has been murdered, Ross is next seen alone with an anonymous 'Old Man' (II.iv) when he speaks freely of events and receives counsel and a blessing. Having returned to Macbeth for the banquet (III.iv), he takes the lead in dealing with his violent reactions on seeing Banquo's ghost. Now, having gone to Scone for Macbeth's coronation (see II.iv.35–6), he has taken a much stronger initiative by going to Fife where he expects to meet Macduff, who has spoken to him about Scotland's future after the murder of Duncan. Finding only his wife and children, all that Ross can do is to counsel patience, show sympathy, and promise to return. Although he achieves little in this scene, his presence shows that the main action of the tragedy contains within its progress the story of this man's loyalties and his slowly developing ability to act with responsible and independent judgement. (See also, the commentary at IV.iii.160–88 and V.vi.74–92).

Lady Macduff's uncomprehending and passionate involvement is likely to make the strongest impression, even with the dismissive 'He had none' (l. 2) and 'Wisdom?' (l. 6). Her gentle love and care become more evident when she considers the 'diminutive' wren and fills the silence left by Ross with a balanced reflection that embraces both her own feelings and those of her husband and their child (l. 27).

Before he leaves, Ross struggles, in a speech of tortured syntax, to speak well of Macduff and give a comprehensive view of the consequences of Macbeth's crime, from which many are suffering as well as themselves. No one in the tragedy has given such a politically conscious account before but his recognition of danger means that he speaks under pressure of time. Before he finishes, he is on the point of tears or some other unwilled and ineffectual breakdown (see ll. 28–30).

**31–64**    Once Lady Macduff is alone with her boy, the verbal and physical style of the play changes radically. Dialogue alternates uncertainly between verse and prose, quick response and silence, and the talk moves between strong personal feeling, large issues, and pert childishness. In performance these exchanges can become indulgently sentimental, mawkish, unbelievable, or even tedious. On the other hand, the change of focus is always assured, despite the uncertainties involved with a very young and necessarily inexperienced actor. In this context, if only a few words ring true, what is said and done is very likely, for a moment at least, to touch instinctive feelings in every spectator.

When saying that the boy's father is dead and was a traitor (ll. 38 and 46), the actor must decide whether the mother believes these replies or not, whether she is preparing her child for the worst possible case or speaking what, at this time, she truly believes, having found no other explanation for what has happened. This decision will colour the entire scene and bring different moments into prominence. Whichever the choice, the dialogue will have a strong subtextual life which her behaviour will sometimes betray and her speech occasionally express in its force or direction.

**65–73**    The unannounced and surprise entry of this anonymous and frightened messenger catapults the action forward and changes everything in an instant. In Shakespeare's time such courage and careful courtesy would have been remarkable in 'a homely man' but no man, however high in social ranking, would break into a lady's privacy so abruptly without quite exceptional cause. Although what he says and does is so circumspect, present-day productions might mark the 'savage' nature of this intruder (l. 70) by his manner of speech, behaviour, or dress. Even if she makes no unscripted sound, Lady Macduff's 'fright' will be plain to see as she clasps her son close.

**73 to the end**     Lady Macduff's question could be addressed to the fleeing messenger but with her next words she speaks for herself, finding that she is caught, like many others in the play, between what she thinks is 'good' and what threatens to destroy her. Remembering that negative virtues are no defence, she sees the need for a courage beyond that expected of her sex. The next moment she is confronted by at least two Murderers – there may be more because they have come to 'slaughter' the entire household. No speech characteristics identify them as the murderers of Act III, scenes i and iii, but in performance they often are and so, very clearly, associated with Macbeth. Because he already knows that Macduff is in England, their opening question is not designed to elicit information but to intimidate and, probably, incriminate.

Although his mother has said his father is a traitor, the boy denies the accusation passionately – to be *shag-haired* was considered the mark of a villain or jailbird – and is immediately stabbed to death, struggling for life long enough to try to save his mother. Her death cries and those of many others are probably heard from off-stage to suggest a general carnage. All this happens very quickly but with utmost brutality, stunning the audience into silence.

## Act IV, scene iii

**1–8**     In modern productions the unprecedented change of location to England will be signalled by a change in lighting and, probably, a set change and new music or sound, but in Shakespeare's day, without these facilities, the surprise would have been effected solely by the actors' performances: the more relaxed voices and behaviour showing that the action has moved away from danger, the signs of a long journey in Macduff's dress and appearance, and the narrative implications of Malcolm's presence.

However staged, the new situation has to be quickly established because, from the start, the dialogue is strained and intentions unclear. Malcolm's opening words are apparently relaxed but are, in fact, a first attempt to test his visitor's intentions, a process that he is prepared to take very much further. Macduff's reply is in a quite different mood and gives a description of Scotland under Macbeth's tyrannous rule. With a new rhythm, Malcolm very briefly, and perhaps curtly, cuts him off.

**9–24**   Malcolm continues to use few words as he gives his reasons for caution, very noticeably speaking only of himself and, more vaguely, of 'the time'. He then openly doubts Macduff's honesty (l. 11), suggesting that he intends to murder the defenceless heir to the Scottish throne. At first Macduff is speechless and only after a half-line pause (l. 17) does he deny the imputation. To this Malcolm again answers briefly at first and then turns to very general and universal considerations: much depends on how he does this.

The actor can present a cold young man who is repeating what he has read in books and is so ignorant of other people that he does not realize how Macduff will be affected by what he says. Alternatively, Malcolm knows very well what he is doing, choosing words carefully and watching the effect of each one. Because this is the first time that Malcolm has held attention so closely, an audience will recognize how exceptional this moment is and he, the young prince as well as the actor, will be well aware that everything hangs on what is about to happen.

A few in the audience may also recognize that Malcolm's reference to the fall of Lucifer is yet another echo of the talk of 'fair' and 'foul' that had introduced both the Witches and Macbeth. This repetition is different in that the idea is firmly situated within well-known Christian narrative and theology.

Again Macduff has little to say but this time he may sound entirely defeated (l. 24): for him, their talk is over. From the start of the scene he may seem unable to think with any subtlety, being either unwilling or unfit to respond to Malcolm's challenges. Alternatively, he may know very well that he is answering the cunning talk of a politician with the forthright and self-sufficient honesty of a soldier.

**25–44**   Although, much later in the scene, Macduff will blame himself for the death of his wife and children (see ll. 223–6), he does not answer when Malcolm says that he distrusts him because he has left them defenceless and 'without leave-taking'. He is so far from thinking of himself and his family that Malcolm's lack of positive response to his plea for help leaves him outraged, fearing for his country and ready to return home. He is held back by Malcolm's reassurance, given in strong and practical terms: a crisis has been avoided.

Shakespeare altered the account given in the *Chronicles*, so that news of Macduff's terrible loss does not reach him until after he has sought Malcolm's help; it is no longer the immediate cause for the journey to England (see p. 109 below). By this change, later in this scene, the audience will *see* the effect that the news has on Macduff and will know for certain that his rebellion against a crowned king is for political and not personal reasons.

**44–103**   Malcolm gives no time for a response to his *volte face* but, with no more than a split second's hesitation, he starts their talk on a new course that will lead Macduff through a series of tests of his potential loyalty. Intellectually and emotionally cornered by what he hears, Macduff struggles to maintain his demand that Malcolm should return to claim the throne by armed insurrection.

What the two men say is so much and so repeatedly at odds, that they may well express their unease by movement across the otherwise empty stage, alternately coming together and parting, sometimes tentatively, sometimes moving quickly and decisively. In this way, their duologue becomes like an engagement in a duel or in a protracted and serious game of hide and seek. Towards its close, some time before line 100, Macduff may be unable to move any more or look his prince in the face. His cry of 'O Scotland, Scotland!' breaking the last of several silences (l. 100), invites a strong physical expression of grief, crossed with frustration and anger.

By adopting this way of bringing the two men together, Shakespeare had also made an opportunity for picturing Scotland's plight under Macbeth's tyranny. By using little more than words for this harrowing aspect of the narrative, he avoided the need to stage an illusion of actual suffering except among Macduff's family. The puzzling nature of this duologue encourages an audience to pay close attention to its account of tyranny and vice.

**101–39**  The actor will not easily find the right tone for Malcolm: he must pretend that he is without hope and yet be seriously concerned. 'I am as I have spoken' is like an actor stopping to say that his performance has been good and true. The difficult moment is soon over because Macduff's passionate outcry of line 100 is not quenched, only deflected. In Trevor Nunn's production at Stratford-upon-Avon in 1976 (see below, pp. 127–30), Macduff turned to face Malcolm and started to strike him, stopped, and then moved away to sob helplessly.

When Macduff continues, the tone becomes very different as he remembers Malcolm's 'most sainted' father and pious mother. After those thoughts have brought a slower, even lingering intensity (ll. 108–11), he is ready to break away from this interview, bitter and hopeless but still passionate (as Malcolm, dropping his pretence, testifies, l. 114). In Holinshed's *Chronicles*, which Shakespeare followed closely in this scene, Macduff weeps 'very abundantly' as he speaks (see p. 111 below).

Malcolm tries many ways to reverse what he has said, including a call for God to 'deal between' them and an account of his very private and personal life (see ll. 124–5), but he gets no response. Even after revealing plans for military action, he has to ask Macduff to say something. He has been speaking to a thoroughly bewildered man, probably sunk low to the ground, head in hands or eyes dazed and lifeless. As the play's action further unfolds, Macduff will be shown to be ready for both words and action when he knows what he should do and say, but here – and later when he hears news of the slaughter of those dearest to him (see ll. 208–10) – his instinct is to hide and be silent. In this Shakespeare altered Holinshed's account, in which the two men immediately ('incontinently') embrace each other as soon as Malcolm confesses to the trick he has played (see p. 112).

Macduff's first words are yet another echo of the theme introduced by the Witches: what is 'fair' can also be 'foul' (see, for example, the last note in the commentary for the previous scene). When someone else comes on stage, Malcolm firmly stops their talk: he is still alert to the risks run by an exiled king, even when among his professed friends.

**140–59** The whole of this episode can be omitted in performance without leaving a gap in the play's narrative or action. The Doctor's unexpected arrival, his ready answer, and Malcolm's informative explanation have led scholars to believe that the entry was a late addition to the play-text. Because the words bear no signs of another author's hand, their inclusion suggests that Shakespeare at least approved of other additions, including that of Hecat in Act III, scene v. The power to heal that 'heaven' has given to the English King acts as a counterbalance to the power that Hecat gives to the Witches. Both episodes extend the boundaries of the play's off-stage space and help to define the energies at work in its plot. The Doctor's talk of King Edward's 'sanctity' (l. 144) echoes what Macduff has recently said about Malcolm's father and mother at lines 108–11.

The episode also relates the play more closely to the England of Shakespeare's day. Malcolm's 'I have seen . . .' gives the effect of an eye-witness account of the healing for the 'King's Evil', which King James, as Edward's heir, had unwillingly 'assayed'. When the episode is retained in present-day performances, it adds a 'miraculous' (l. 147) element to the status of royalty and gives further credence to 'prophecy' (l. 157).

By interrupting the action at a crucial and emotional point, replacing a strong and very verbal development with an equally verbal digression that is informative and reflective, any tension that has built up will be lost as the audience is led to take a wider view before the next major development in the play's action. While Malcolm has been speaking enthusiastically and with reverence about the English king, Macduff has been silent and, perhaps, more watchful or less absorbed because, this time, it is he who first sees a new arrival.

**160–88** Ross has changed. He is no longer an official messenger or someone giving a personal and last-minute warning (see 'I dare not speak much further', IV.ii.17). His arrival in England is timely, the initiative his own, and his purpose assured. Nevertheless he says almost nothing at first. Warmly greeted, he has nothing to say to Macduff and only the briefest possible reply to Malcolm. When asked directly about Scotland, his account, as Macduff says, is both shockingly 'true' and nicely expressed (l. 174). Actors often deliver these words as if they have been rehearsed and yet, even so, the speech will lose forward energy towards the end when Ross speaks of flowers in dead men's caps.

Asked for more precise news, Ross prevaricates. The theatre audience knows very well what he is holding back, until Macduff's more general question 'How goes't?' allows him to escape from 'niggard' speech and turn to the hopeful news he has brought and a call for present action, which he addresses to Malcolm. Macduff's short-phrased personal questions add to the pressure that Ross must feel from his unspoken news. The three men, alone on the stage, are likely to shift in stance and in gaze while the audience is made to wait for an outcome that it knows must come. This close focus on two almost tongue-tied men uniquely emphasizes this moment in the play's action and prepares for its most sustained presentation of personal loss and suffering.

**188–210**   Malcolm's up-beat words to Ross relieve the ominous mood but he responds in a different key with a promise of yet more terrifying news. The words that Macduff prises from him only postpone what he has to say until he bluntly gives the news that the theatre audience has been expecting. Macduff's answer is an appalled silence. He probably stays stone still until he pulls his hat down onto his brow in an attempt to hide a deeper and more total convulsion than Malcolm's well-meaning advice can alleviate.

**211–34**   Knowing the pain his words are inflicting, when Macduff's brief question forces him to repeat what has already been said, Ross falls silent. When Malcolm takes over, his advice is counterproductive, leading Macduff to expose his raw feelings, which now include a sense of his own complicity (see ll. 223–6) as well as his anger against the 'hell-kite' who ordered the atrocity.

'He has no children' can be said about Malcolm, who has offered only conventional encouragement, or, with a greater jump in consciousness, these words can refer to Macbeth, on whom his thoughts will certainly focus two lines later before reverting, more vividly and more tenderly, to his appalling loss. The movement in his consciousness has become as expressive as his words, perhaps more so as his body bears each successive wrench. 'I shall do so' is more certainly a reproof to Malcolm and marks a turning point in the scene as Macduff takes a stronger hold on his words, which now turn to 'heaven', a word that seems to stand for God as well as an implacable Fate.

With 'Heaven rest them now' (l. 225), Macduff seems to find some consolation even as he comes close to tears (see l. 229). Then, again, he moves forward to commit himself to punitive action while, still, keeping heaven in view – now, a superhuman and revenging providence that is, ironically, the '*gentle* heavens'.

**234 to the end**    Malcolm, as heir to his father's throne, takes charge firmly and comprehensively. Rhymes and assertions, piety and proverbial wisdom, express a common resolve as everyone leaves the stage.

# ACT V

## Act V, scene i

**1–20**    As soon as the three men have left, united in warlike purpose, a second Doctor and an unnamed Gentlewoman enter apprehensively. After the ringing couplet that concluded the previous scene, these people stay together, speaking anxiously in prose. There is a sense of mystery or uncertainty because this is the third time they have 'watched' at night together and, so far, the Doctor has seen nothing to confirm the woman's report of her mistress, Lady Macbeth. He listens as she gives details of her sleepwalking and then comments knowledgeably until his second question immediately changes the contact between the two: she is afraid to answer and refuses to do so. From what she now says it becomes clear that she has brought the Doctor to this place – somewhere unspecified in the castle – to both see and hear what may be about to happen so that her earlier reports will be believed and a highly dangerous secret shared. Nothing like this has come before in the play; the only extended prose episode has been with the Porter at the castle gate in the early morning, its mood not obviously anxious or strained (II.iii).

At this moment Lady Macbeth enters carrying a lighted '*taper*' (a Folio stage direction). The voices of the watchers will drop and, on 'stand close' (l. 20), they will move aside to be less conspicuous – even though the sleepwalker sees nothing and they are protected by the darkness of night. Even in the unvarying light of the play's earliest performances, they may have put their own lights out to enhance the appearance of darkness, lit only by Lady Macbeth's taper.

**21–30**    After taking control of the chaotic events that followed the appearances of Banquo's ghost, Lady Macbeth said very little while still on stage (III.iv.121–43), and, since then, she has not been seen. Now her silence is absolute so that her actions and appearance will draw the audience's closest attention, while concentrating on her face, which is lit by the one flickering taper on the open space of the stage. Among all the entries of this action-driven play, none has been so isolated or made in such a protracted silence. Preparation for it has been careful and now the two watchers provide a commentary on what the audience is witnessing.

After entering, Lady Macbeth must in some way dispose of the light in order to wash her hands (see l. 29). This means that her attempt to cleanse herself will be seen as a deliberate act and not an unthinking reflex. At the time when the play was written a taper might well be fixed into a wrought-iron stand, in which it could be carried or placed down anywhere at will.

**31–42**    'Yet here's a spot' probably implies that the hand-washing has been continuing for some time off stage and is vigorous, or possibly frenzied. These few words will also take the thoughts of an audience back to the time after the murder when Macbeth was appalled at the blood on his hands and his wife showed no fear, believing that 'A little water clears us of this deed' (II.ii.59–68).

As Lady Macbeth's words come more freely, it is clear that she is re-living the murder, as well as its aftermath, and that her husband is constantly in her mind. But two phrases are unlike any earlier words and seem to come unbidden and without any specific preparation. The first, 'Hell is murky,' carries a sensuous awareness of continuing punishment in a supernatural existence. The second is also sensuous and expresses an appalled memory of Duncan's bleeding corpse, now that of 'the old man', which the actor, if not the audience, is bound to link to Lady Macbeth's equally surprising excuse before the murder, 'Had he not resembled / My father as he slept, I had done't' (II.ii.12–13). These thoughts imply that Lady Macbeth's sleep-freed consciousness is hypersensitive and her entire being alert beyond any ordinary or everyday awareness.

After a silence that allows time for the Doctor's brief comment (he will be taking notes while she is speaking; see ll. 32–3), Lady Macbeth remembers Macduff's wife as if conscious of her equal status as a thane's wife (see l. 41). Sufficient time has passed for Macbeth to have gone 'into the field' of battle (l. 4) but it is not clear whether his wife knows that his opponent's wife and children have been 'savagely slaughtered' (IV.ii.205). Perhaps her mind has travelled into the future before coming back to blood-stained hands and the fear that had incapacitated her husband. As she reproves him she again becomes silent, having no more to say; perhaps she is now immobile, as her husband had been, and has stopped washing her hands.

**46–57**    The watchers have time to register the consequences of what talking in sleep has betrayed. In alarm, the Doctor addresses the somnambulist, who cannot hear, presumably drawn by the intensity of her words to respond as if she were fully conscious. The Gentlewoman now has the witness she needed (see ll. 17–18) but remains apprehensive of what more may be said.

From Lady Macbeth's reference to her hand, it seems that the rubbing has stopped and she has brought one hand towards her face to test whether the smell alone would betray the murder. That action then brings the 'perfumes of Arabia' to mind and a sense of the small-ness of her own hand, two contrasting thoughts that so extend her self-awareness that she lets out a three times repeated cry, wordless and seeming to come from deep within her physical being – from her 'heart' and affecting her 'whole body' (ll. 51–2). The comments it draws mark this as the most shattering moment of the sleepwalking: the Doctor immediately contrasts this patient with those who have had peaceful deaths, as if he believes Lady Macbeth is about to die.

**58–66**  After a silence, which could accompany an attempt to wrestle with physical and mental pressures, Lady Macbeth's response is to take charge of her husband, giving short and practical directions as if he were present. Denying that Macbeth had seen a ghost, she tells him that Banquo could never return to haunt him. A moment's hesitation at this point would allow time for the Doctor's question before she drops the argument and calls repeatedly for him to come to bed. Having offered her hand, she again tries to argue, this time accepting what they both have experienced beyond all doubt (see I.vii.1 and III.ii.12).

She probably leaves the stage as if holding his hand and drawing him to follow. Her words are the last she utters in the play and they can be played in many ways: as if needing his fellowship or his physical and sexual presence; or, quite differently, as if taking control is her last resource or, perhaps, the last thing she can think of. If she remembers that he cannot sleep without having terrifying dreams, her insistence that he follow will be for concealment, not for the comfort that sleep can bring. If she has forgotten this, her thoughts must be chiefly of her own needs.

The Doctor's question that follows suggests an element of uncertainty in whatever the exit expresses. The Gentlewoman's response shows that, however deep the suffering of this sleepwalking, it is one in a sequence of similar occasions. An actor would have difficulty in picking up and holding the taper while leaving with an imaginary Macbeth and so her attendant will probably do so, an action that will again show that this has been no exceptional event.

**67 to the end**  The Doctor's closing speech is very like a soliloquy in which he shares what he is thinking with the audience. It also functions like a formal Chorus by widening the context in which the foregoing action is viewed and by using familiar proverbs to ensure understanding. The prayer to 'God' for forgiveness (l. 71) – a rare use of that word in this text – makes common cause with everyone in the audience. The brief and sensible orders that follow draw the scene to an 'amazed', swift, and apprehensive conclusion.

## Act V, scene ii

**1–11**   When listening to Lady Macbeth's fragmented and allusive words in the preceding scene, the audience must have stayed attentive in order to understand; otherwise they would remain puzzled and, to some extent, excluded from what was happening on stage. Now, in contrast, drum, flags, and marching soldiers, followed by direct and stirring speeches, make the new situation completely clear. Lennox, who was last seen attending Macbeth in the previous Act, and Angus, not seen since he was Duncan's messenger in Act I, are joined by two thanes who are making their first appearance in the play: the narrative has obviously taken a large step forward. If Angus points off stage, over the heads of most of the audience, as he announces, 'That way they are coming,' the silent reactions of his fellow thanes as they look in that direction will give a sense of impending reinforcements and good fortune.

**11–28**   Cathness gives the first of three responses to Menteth's question. His reference to Macbeth, not by name but as 'the tyrant', is Shakespeare's concentrated way of alluding to the many cruelties and injustices which *The Chronicles* recount as taking place over a number of years. The account of fortifying Dunsinane 'strongly' suggests that Shakespeare had in mind Holinshed's description of its site on a steep hill and the forced labour by which Macbeth attempted to make it impregnable (see p. 108 below).

Talk of Macbeth's madness and 'pestered senses' takes attention away from the present situation until the resolve, 'march we on', and a call to purge Scotland's sickness by a sacrificial loss of lives, draw the scene to an end in common action.

**29–31**   Lennox's restrained agreement marks still further his
increasing weight as a thane. The metaphor of a 'sovereign' (i.e. healing) flower and 'weed' is reminiscent of *Richard II* (Act III, scene iv) and
*Hamlet* (I.ii.135–7) and brings the entire future of Scotland to mind.
The assured couplet may be answered with unscripted cries of affir-
mation and confidence. The metrically incomplete line that follows
sends everyone '*marching*' off stage (Folio stage direction), presumably
as they had entered, with drum accompaniment and flags held high.

### Act V, scene iii

**1–18**   Macbeth's short and contrasted phrases require an energetic
and rapid entry onto the stage. No indication is given of why he
enters or to what place in his castle he has come but his reliance on
the Witches' prophecies is soon made very clear, and repeatedly so.
His denial of any 'taint' of fear and denigration of his enemies may
lead the actor to give a less than full confidence to this opening
speech: much will depend on how strong he has shown Macbeth's
imagination to be and how prevalent his power to deceive himself.

However the opening has been played, when a servant enters
unannounced with fear written all over him, the vaunting king and
commander curses him with disproportionate fury before this
anonymous messenger is able to speak a word. When the 'patch'
[*fool*] fails to say what soldiers they are, Macbeth rebukes him, saying
his entrance has already awakened the fear he had earlier denied.

**19–29**   An incomplete verse-line indicates a silence after the servant
identifies an 'English force'. In this moment Macbeth changes and
makes one of the numerous and rapid transitions of mood that char-
acterize his appearances in the last Act. Dismissing the messenger
without giving him another thought, he calls for Seyton (who has
neither entered nor been mentioned before) and then, without waiting for a response, he confesses to an inward sickness and weakness.
Reiterating and emphasizing his call for Seyton, he reverts to previously hidden thoughts, confessing to the peril that he feels himself to
be in, having gained the throne (alluded to now, less dangerously, as

a 'chair' and 'seat'). He looks back, rather than forward, expressing longingly his thoughts of what might have been, the permanent value that the 'imperial theme' had promised (I.iii.128).

An audience will probably see Macbeth stand still, as if a ship that has been beached or an aircraft that has stalled, until he proceeds to speak of the hatred and fear his subjects feel towards him. His courage and very sinews will have shrivelled before their eyes. Only another call for Seyton shows that he has engaged once more in the present. This is either a very short line or else a non-metrical one: in the silence or disruption that this implies, he either summons his courage or waits for this necessary person to enter. Some members of the audience at early performances may have heard the name as 'Satan' and so believe that the call must be heard in hell before bringing an awesome response. In any event, the delay before Seyton appears will suggest that he is a wilful, brooding, or highly independent person: it may be thought that he, like the thanes before him, has abandoned his master.

**30–48**　　When Seyton eventually appears, he speaks with a courtesy that is in strong contrast to every other speech in this scene. He seems in control, especially when he ignores Macbeth's talk of hacking flesh to tell him that armour is 'not needed yet'. In turn Macbeth now ignores Seyton and, after a half-line's pause, gives orders in brutal disregard of the fear that he knows is rife among those troops that remain – as it is, or has very recently been, in himself.

While putting on his armour he sees the Doctor, who is standing among the remaining soldiers and, like them, watching silently. Either he has remembered his sick wife, or happening to turn towards the Doctor brings that thought to mind. This is one of the many small decisions that the actor will have to make, according to the nature of the bond that has developed between husband and wife in the course of the play. Hearing of her sleeplessness, Macbeth's feelings and mood change yet again so that when he speaks of 'perilous stuff' weighing on the heart the Doctor answers as if Macbeth were the patient, who needs to 'minister to *him*-self'. The pause that follows is probably so terror-struck that the sudden surge of vocal and physical energy as Macbeth seeks to lose himself in action is likely to be literally breathtaking.

**49–60**    With his attention divided between the presence of the Doctor and arming himself – or briefly, at line 54, starting to disarm since 'Pull't off' could refer to an article of either clothing or armour – Macbeth is drawn to speak of the thanes who have deserted him and the disease afflicting what he calls 'my land'. Again wishing for what he knows to be impossible, for the 'honour, love, obedience, troops of friends' that he has lost forever (l. 25), he is caught and helpless. And again he seeks a remedy for fear and finds it in courage and action (see ll. 32–3), backed up now by trust in what the Witches have prophesied. He leaves at once, not saying where he is going and, probably, so rapidly that his '*Attendants*' are left to follow after.

**61–2**    This short soliloquy offers the entirely different perspective of a learned man who is afraid to stay where he practises his skill and knowledge. As he stands alone before leaving, the contrast to Macbeth could hardly be greater or of more import.

### Act V, scene iv

**1–to the end**    The entry repeats that of scene ii, with its drum and colours, but with Malcolm, Macduff and Seyward at the head of the soldiers, the narrative has moved on and the mood is more assured. The audience will know – as no one on stage can know – that Malcolm's battle-orders will, in a quibbling sense, fulfil one of the Witches' prophecies from Act IV, scene ii – the one in which Macbeth has just placed his trust (see V.iii.59–60). It will now watch activity that already has the promise of success stamped upon it.

Seyward gives the order to proceed with the authority of a clear mind and the experience of an older man. If he speaks with a different, more English accent and wears different fighting gear and markings, he will also signify the greater resources of Malcolm's army. This scene is shorter than Act V, scene ii, the change giving an impression of gathering impetus.

## Act V, scene v

**1–7**     Although Macbeth's opening words are still defiant and in the imperative mood, their phrasing suggests a slower tempo than that of his last entry. He has decided to rely on his castle's defences rather than meet and engage with his enemy and, in saying so, he registers another loss besides that of the thanes who have deserted him, a loss of active fighting that is shaming for 'Bellona's bridegroom' (I.ii.56). Yet he remains alert to an off-stage sound and asks its cause with sufficient sharpness to send Seyton off to enquire its source without delay.

**8–15**     Perhaps Macbeth has guessed what the noise is, as Seyton has. He does not reply directly to what he is told but is absorbed in his own reaction to it and, from that, in his recent experiences. Introspection, taking the place of action, leads him to declare himself insensitive to fear because he is sated with 'horrors' and his own 'slaughterous thoughts'. Nevertheless he questions the returning Seyton before he can deliver his news.

**16–28**     Two incomplete verse-lines indicate more than one pause or silence, and consequently call for thoughtful and deeply felt speech. Seyton could scarcely speak more simply but Macbeth's 'died' joins the present loss with the less tense and demanding 'hereafter'. This leads him to reflect on what he takes to be a common experience of the past and of life's ultimate destination. Shakespeare has put the narrative on hold so that the audience is able to view the persons of the play as unremarkable men and women engaged in a brief performance like that of an actor. To do this through the mouthpiece of the tragic hero is to give him the function of a Chorus, which prompts his audience to revalue all that is happening on stage. With 'full of sound and fury', however, the impassioned and brutal action of the play comes back to mind in terms that have become natural to Macbeth and separate him from everyone else – only to be dismissed as meaningless.

**29–41**   The change to an impatient demand for news contradicts
Macbeth's assertion that life is a tale that signifies 'nothing'.
Instinctively, he *does* need to know what the frightened entry means
and this brings about yet another instantaneous change of mood. The
messenger speaks with several starts and hesitations, not expecting to
be believed, and anticipates punishment when his news is told.
Macbeth must hold himself sufficiently in check for the man to repeat,
more succinctly, what he has said before. Taking this in, Macbeth
bursts out with threats of an immediate and slow death should the
news be false, picturing that torture precisely. In this moment he
contemplates his defeat and knows that, if it does happen, he would
accept the same punishment for himself, careless of anything else. His
mind has come back to the nothing of an idiot's tale.

**42 to the end**   Returning to his present predicament, Macbeth
dramatizes the situation so that he sees what he does while he is
doing it. Beginning to 'doubt' [*fear, distrust*] the Witches' message as
the lying trick of 'the fiend' (by this he probably means the devil
himself, who can quote scripture for his own purposes; see *The
Merchant of Venice*, I.iii.97–101, 178), he nevertheless still takes refuge in
action, calling on his remaining followers to 'Arm, arm, and out!'
Changing from a defensive strategy, he is now ready to meet his
enemies, 'direful, beard to beard' (V.v.6).

Couplets serve to emphasize the conclusion of the scene, including lines 49 and 50 which counter-state his committal to action with
a weariness and disillusion that wishes for the end of the known
world, not victory in battle. He goes to fight torn inwardly between
the defeat he can foresee and what he must now do in consequence
of the decisions he has made and the man he has become. An audience will sense that the play is approaching its end but how the tragic
hero will confront his last moments is not yet determined.

### Act V, scene vi

**1–10**   During the course of the next 210 lines, which are often
printed as one continuous final scene (as in the New Penguin edition,

followed in this commentary), the stage is repeatedly empty while 'alarums' are variously called for in the Folio text. Some editions, notably the Oxford/Norton edition (1988), mark a new scene on each of these occasions, giving a total of six separate scenes that end with Act V, scene xi; the New Cambridge edition (1997) has a total of four scenes, ending with Act V, scene ix on Malcolm's last entry. The Folio has just one new scene, after line 10. What is not controversial, and apparent in any editorial arrangement, is that the coming and going of armed men, accompanied by the sound of fighting and military engagement, together with one rapid and one prolonged fight to the death, provide a sequence of physical, aural, and wordless episodes that occur between short verbal passages, some of them highly charged with emotion. In performance the effect is often that of a rush of contrary events that spill over into off-stage space, and of the passing of time at varying and uncertain speeds. Even in the last episode, with almost the whole company of actors on stage, much more is about to happen and has happened than is shown to the audience: see, for example, the soldiers who salute Malcolm 'in their minds', and Malcolm's list of 'What's more to do' and his 'thanks to all at once' (ll. 95–6, 103, and 113).

All the fragments in this staging are held together by the strong and often intense focus that is repeatedly drawn to Macbeth in the last episodes of his life while he confronts his fate and discovers the last resources of his mind and body – all that he has been and all that can now be called his. Other persons command attention but none for long or with any comparable revelation. The most effective counterbalance to the presentation of the play's hero is the gathering of determined opponents, their thoughts for the future of Scotland, the fulfilment of the Witches' prophecies, and the workings of providence or what Malcolm calls 'the grace of Grace' (l. 111).

The final sequence of events starts with 'Drum and colours' and the entry of Macbeth's leading opponents, very much as before except that they are accompanied by an 'army', which is half-hidden by the green boughs they carry. This strange visual effect needs careful stage-management; not least in early performances when entry to the stage was from a crowded (and probably dark) tiring house and through two small doors, with or without the use of a central and wider opening. Today, with a small company of actors in a theatre with little technical equipment, the effect is in danger of looking ridiculous. Often the army is addressed as if it were off stage and out of sight, a solution of the difficulty that is easy to manage but loses a striking visual fulfilment of the Witches' prophecy and a symbolic representation of renewed life and the natural resources of the country (see p. 158 below).

Malcolm gives orders briefly and they are received with instant and unspoken agreement. Only Seyward has a word of farewell before battle, followed by a couplet that speaks for the army's readiness to fight the tyrant. Macduff's couplet concludes the episode, charged by his personal resolve and calling for trumpets to clamour for 'blood and death' – an acceptance of violence and retributive fate.

If staged at all fully, the army's exit will be almost as complicated as its entrance, and take as long. Presumably, every available trumpet should sound to represent the widespread and open rebellion that faces the king. The Folio's direction, '*Alarms continued*', reads like an instruction to modulate the trumpets into more general sounds of military activity, perhaps with orders given and sounds of manoeuvring soldiers. A clash of weapons would be less appropriate because victory will prove to be 'cheaply won' (l. 76), and yet, somehow, stage-sound should represent the siege of the castle by thousands of soldiers. Neither it nor the trumpets are all that 'speak' for the approaching war: Macbeth's words and physical presence on his entry, which immediately follows, are likely to be a more compelling sign of what is about to happen.

**11–23**    Chained bears being set upon by dogs provided a spectator sport that was popular with all classes of Londoners, even though blood was spilt and its cruelty obvious. Beyond this image, the only indication of the off-stage progress of the siege is that Macbeth believes himself to be all but invincible. He may feel sufficiently secure to laugh as he remembers what the Witches have told him (see ll. 22–3 and V.v.2–3).

When young Seyward enters ready for combat, Macbeth answers his challenge laconically, perhaps with a touch of pity for the young man's ignorance. After an easy victory, Macbeth leaves, elated and still more convinced of the efficacy of prophecy. If Hecat has been included earlier in the play, some in the audience may recall her words at the conclusion of her speech:

> . . . you all know security
> Is mortals' chiefest enemy.
>
> (III.v.32–3)

Some editions add a stage direction requiring Macbeth to carry off the corpse, but an actor is likely to find little motive for Macbeth to tidy the stage; any anonymous soldier could find a later opportunity to do the job inconspicuously, especially if a number of supernumeraries cross and re-cross the stage during some of the alarms.

**24–33**   With sounds of battle before and after, Macduff briefly holds the stage, an isolated figure with his every thought centred on Macbeth's crimes and cruelty. He shows no signs that he has been fighting, on either body or clothes, and his sword shines, for it is as yet unused. He is alert and ready, his breath steady. He leaves as soon as increased 'clatter' from the battle (l. 31) makes him think he knows where the tyrant can be found and killed.

**34–9**   In what will prove the shortest episode between the alarums of this scene, Seyward enters with Malcolm, both of them confident and unhurried. As they leave, the accompanying sound may change into a trumpet call signalling an advance. The Folio stage direction does not specify soldiers in attendance, but they are usually provided to add authority to the presence of these two leaders and to give a physical representation of the castle's capture. However, Shakespeare may have used a sequence of brief scenes with only a few persons on stage in order to highlight their contrasted natures and enable the entire conflict to be presented with deliberate speed and without taking too much attention from the main business of the tragedy's conclusion (see the commentary at the beginning of this scene).

**40–7**   Rarely in the play and nowhere else in the last Act does Macbeth enter asking a question and there is no need for editors to mark one here, the punctuation of the Folio text being no more authoritative here than elsewhere. The words to be spoken would be appropriate as a bragging exclamation, not a question, and so lead without pause into a merciless threat of slaughter. Played this way, Macduff's 'hellhound' would be particularly appropriate. However, some actors play this entry as a moment of introspection and doubt. If he has seriously considered the possibility of suicide, Macbeth's frame of mind would lend weight to what he says about his troubled 'soul' (ll. 44–5).

Macduff's entry from behind Macbeth suddenly reconfigures the stage and brings about the long anticipated confrontation. Macbeth at once remembers the warning of the first of the apparitions, 'beware Macduff!' (IV.i.70–1), and then the slaughter of this man's family, which he had ordered. How far these thoughts shake or shatter his confidence will depend on the actor's instincts and conscious choices earlier in the play, all modified by how the performance has developed as it has unfolded. The audience's reaction to the entire tragedy will be strongly influenced by what this moment reveals of Macbeth's innermost and instinctive thoughts. It is only a brief, though crucial, moment because Macduff insists on fighting at once.

**47–73**    The sharing of line 47 between two men who are fighting to the death suggests that this first exchange takes only a little time. Indeed, Macbeth might speak between blows without stopping the fight because at this point he can be full of confidence. The most sudden and unforeseeable interruption comes after the short line 55. Hearing it Macbeth is devastated: after a silence for the words to sink in, he can only respond with a curse and blame for the 'fiends' who have deceived him. His next thought is to avoid the encounter but as he listens to Macduff's taunts he becomes more sure of himself and accepts that death is the only future that he can accept and remain true to his instinctive belief in action (see, for example, the Commentary on IV.i.234ff., V.iii.50–60, V.v.42ff.). Courage, self-protection, pride, authority, will-power, appetite for dominance, longing for kingly graces – any of the various impulses that have led him through the action of the play – can resurface here. As the fight is resumed and continues Macbeth is fully exposed for all the inner worth with which the text and performance have endowed him.

The Folio stage direction has been variously represented by editors, and the fighting on and off stage still more variously handled by actors and, in recent times, by fight directors, play directors, and light and sound designers. The one aspect that is constant from one production to another is that one of the actors has played a much smaller part in the preceding action than the other. The weight of the long and varied central role makes this last testing of Macbeth a formidable test for the actor. His acceptance of the challenge, when near exhaustion and facing a fresh and powerful adversary, becomes part of what the audience experiences in the last moments of the tragic hero. Any present-day actor worthy of the role will want, against all odds, to finish the play with what Laurence Olivier once called 'a hell of a good fight'. When sword-fighting was a more common accomplishment this was probably an even more crucial encounter and, possibly, the reason why the Folio text directs the two men to leave the stage fighting and return almost at once to continue fighting until one of them is dead. For an alternative explanation, see p. 157 below.

**74–92**   A '*Retreat and flourish*' on trumpets mark Malcolm's victory and '*drum and colours*' bring the maximum possible number of actors on stage in military order. The mood is restrained, awaiting further news, and it will deepen when Ross steps forward to report what he knows. On this last of the four occasions when Ross brings bad news, he seems fully prepared and ready to help its recipient. With dramatic focus brought, and held, upon Seyward, his stoicism, heroic ideals, and religious faith are in strong contrast to every other sentiment in the final Act. The incident is found in Holinshed (see pp. 113–14) but the place and prominence it has been given in the plot of this tragedy is entirely Shakespeare's doing.

**93 to the end**   Holinshed reports that Macbeth's head was displayed on a pole (see p. 113) and this is usual stage practice today. (But see p. 129, below, for an alternative.) Macduff now speaks to the entire company on stage and his words are followed by a general acclamation of Malcolm as king, and other less formal or vocal signs of triumph. For him the 'usurper's cursèd head' is sufficient obsequy for his opponent but other thoughts will also be present in the audience's mind in so far as individual members have been affected by Macbeth's journey through the play and, more especially, by his last moments when he faces certain death. So, too, when Malcolm speaks of 'this dead butcher and his fiend-like queen' (l. 108), the reactions of some in the audience to both persons will be acknowledged, but by no means those of everyone. A gap has opened up between the feelings of persons in the play who stand victorious and relieved on the stage and the responses of at least some members of the audience. By opposing the words of the moment to the audience's experience of the whole play, the young and unscathed Malcolm to the tested and still fighting Macbeth, Shakespeare has ensured that everyone watching the play makes his or her own judgement on its conclusion.

Malcolm's concluding speech does not 'spend a large expense of time' (l. 99) in dealing with its many significant matters and looking forward to his and the nation's future. He speaks with an efficiency that can be chilling rather than reassuring to those who hear him. After a passing reference to God (l. 111), the new king soon leaves ahead of the others, who are now his subjects and invited to his coronation. Yet again the trumpets sound and the stage empties, except, perhaps, for the severed and bloody head raised on a pole in much the same manner as the heads of traitors were displayed in Shakespeare's day at the southern entrance to London Bridge where they were left to rot.

# 3 The Play's Sources and Cultural Context

When writing *Macbeth*, Shakespeare drew principally on Raphael Holinshed's *Chronicles of England, Scotland and Ireland*, but a reader or actor approaching the text today will be aware of matters whose sources can seldom be identified with any certainty. Witches with prophetic powers are unfamiliar to us, and so are the ghost and airborne dagger, belief in the efficacy of prayer and divine providence, and the right of a monarch to administer justice and exercise an absolute power. Many details of daily life in the Scotland and England of the early eleventh century, the time of the historical Macbeth, were very different from those of our own time and culture and some would have been strange to Shakespeare's contemporaries. All these elements in the tragedy may be better understood in the light of its possible sources and other writings that were widely read at the time.

## The two kingdoms of James I

For Holinshed, Scotland of the eleventh century was barbarous and constantly ravaged by warfare as it was attacked from abroad and divided within. William Harrison's *Description of Britain*, reprinted as an introduction to *The Chronicles* and going further back in time, calls the earliest Scots 'the most Scythian-like and the most barbarous nation, and the longest without letters'. Fostered by repeated battles and cross-border raids, this reputation lingered on, at least until the accession of James VI to England as James I brought the security of a settled lineage to both countries. Yet, even then, suspicions remained and it was an uneasy 'union' that held the two monarchies together.

When the King's Men performed *The Tragedy of Gowrie* in 1604 the

play had to be withdrawn after two performances: its text has not
survived but the Earl of Gowrie was known for his attempted assassination of James, four years earlier. In comedies, hostility to the
Scots became a subject for satire, mostly aimed at the influence they
had gained at Court, which was then the seat of government and
source of all major preferment in the country. For some years the
Scots remained a dangerous subject to air in public. For a passing
criticism in the comedy *Eastward Ho!* (1605), two of its authors, George
Chapman and Ben Jonson, were imprisoned. In *The Merchant of Venice*
as first published in 1600, Portia tells how a Scottish suitor, having
had his ears boxed by an Englishman, swore to 'pay him again when
he was able' (I.ii.78) but even this comment had become risky after
James's accession and in the First Folio of 1623 'Scottish suitor' was
changed to the inoffensive and uninteresting 'the other suitor.' In
these circumstances, the choice of a Scottish monarch for a tragic
hero was not without danger in 1606. Perhaps that was one reason
for embellishing the story as found in the *Chronicles* with the apparitions, which introduced visible and verbal evidence that it was
Banquo, and not the regicide Macbeth, who was the ancestor of
James I.

The first Stuart king encouraged some controversies by published
writings. His 'instructions to his dearest son' in *Basilikon Doron* of 1599
were many times reprinted and translated after 1603. This treatise
reflects the view of Niccolo Machiavelli in *The Prince* (1531) that a
ruler's actions 'must be tempered by humanity and prudence' (xvii)
and that authority should be exercised with regard to expediency,
rather than strictly moral considerations. The nature of kings and of
government were to become very live issues at the start of the seventeenth century as James struggled to exert his will against a newly
assertive House of Commons. By 1610 its 'Grievances' had become so
frequent that he went to Whitehall to address both Houses of
Parliament. There he declared that 'kings are justly called gods' and
that it was 'sedition in subjects to dispute what a king may do in the
height of his power'. He warned members not to 'meddle with such
ancient rights of mine, as I have received from my predecessors. . . .
All novelties are dangerous as well in a politic as in a natural body.'

In Holinshed Shakespeare found a stark contrast between a

Duncan who was too temperate to be a king, by nature given to holiness and generosity, and a Macbeth who was too aggressive, by nature being cruel and ruthless (see below, p. 103). This dichotomy he modified, having an older Duncan who, according to Macbeth, has 'borne his faculties so meek' that angels will plead 'trumpet-tongued' against his murder (I.vii.16–20), and with a Macbeth who at the start 'disdain[s] fortune' in battle and wreaks 'bloody execution' on Duncan's enemies. Current debates about the qualities needed in a ruler surface later in Act IV, scene iii, a long scene that is usually severely cut in present-day productions. Here Malcolm lists 'justice, verity, temperance, stableness, / Bounty, perseverance' among the kingly graces (ll. 91–4) while, at the same time, cunningly concealing his own intentions. These concerns are also present but in a very different light when Macbeth recognizes that, by his crimes, he has forfeited the 'honour, love, obedience, troops of friends' that a king should possess (V.iii.24–8). Politically *The Tragedy of Macbeth* belongs to a time when the king's authority was being challenged progressively and the House of Commons was about to become the breeding ground for civil war. Shakespeare was in a position to be very aware of this when his fellow actors performed at Court, as they frequently did in revivals of his plays. While there, he would have opportunity, in anterooms and corridors, to hear talk of immediate public interest about English politics that, as 'matters of state', could not be treated openly in plays.

At the beginning of Act II, scene iii, the Porter, who has drunk too much the night before, does voice common concerns of the early seventeenth century such as the price of food in a time of inflation and the accompanying dangers of speculation. He also exemplifies a perceived need for the new 'Act to restrain the inordinate Haunting and Tippling in Inns, Alehouses, and other Victualling Houses' that the parliamentary *Journals* for 1604 record passing through both Houses of Parliament. The Porter's welcome for an 'equivocator' who has 'committed treason for God's sake' is best understood as a reference to the Jesuit Father Garnet, who gave false evidence in court in an attempt to escape the death sentence for his leading part in the Gunpowder Plot against the king and parliament. Later in the play, Macbeth's long interrogation of two committed cut-throats shows

Shakespeare's awareness of dangerous discontent among those who were 'masterless men' in an unsettled and unjust world (III.i.90).


## Witchcraft

The Witches who open the tragedy and increasingly influence Macbeth are without parallel in Shakespeare's other plays. Difficult to represent on stage in a believable way today, their presence would have been more familiar but also problematic when the play was first performed, the nature and power of witches being debated even while persons convicted witchcraft were being pilloried, imprisoned, hanged, or burnt alive. In rural areas, so-called witches might be laughed at or visited for minor cures and fortune telling and yet, in courts of law, the practice of witchcraft was a capital offence.

To the controversy that arose throughout Europe, the king had contributed a book, *Demonology*, which was published in 1597 and then twice reprinted in 1603. As its title page announces, he set out to prove from scripture, learned writings, and current reports that the 'unlawful arts' of witches 'have been and may be put in practice' and the book argues that this should be prosecuted and punished. It describes their 'circles and conjurations' and their claims to have contracts with the Devil. By such means, they were reputed to become invisible, transport themselves to distant places, and work their will over chosen victims. Female witches are reported to outnumber males by twenty to one because, 'as that sex is frailer than man is, so it is easier to be intrapped in these gross snares of the Devil' (I.v). Although nowhere in *Macbeth* is witchcraft clearly associated with the devil – theatre being forbidden to deal with matters of religion – the suggestion is there (see the commentary on V.v.43 and V.vi.58–61) and some among Shakespeare's audiences, seeing the witches 'vanish' and hearing of their flight through the air (whether that was staged or not), may well have believed that they were evil spirits or humans possessed by spirits (see I.i.10, I.iii.79–81, and IV.i.131 s.d. and 137). The fulfilment of their riddling prophecies may well have been understood in the same way or, as Holinshed suggests, by thinking of them as 'goddesses of destiny', nymphs or fairies, or 'creatures of [an] elder world' (see p. 105 below). Undoubtedly witches were feared by many of Shakespeare's contemporaries, a few of whom would have been amazed or terrified when seeing them on stage. The title page of a pamphlet of 1594 gives a taste of current attitudes: '*The most strange and admirable discovery of the three witches of Warboys, arraigned, convicted and executed at the last assizes at Huntington.*'

Two substantial books had been published on the other side of the argument. Reginald Scot's *Discovery of Witchcraft* (1584) sets out to prove that 'the compacts and contracts of witches with devils and all infernal spirits or familiars are but erroneous novelties and imaginary conceptions' (title page). Scot describes the 'juggling tricks' of supposed witches and quotes Geoffrey Chaucer's denunciation of the 'knavery' of priests who spread a fear of them and the belief that evil spirits lurked 'in every bush, and under every tree' (IV.xii). Samuel Harsnett's *Declaration of egregious Popish Impostures* (1603) describes how so-called witches faked demonic possession; it was here that Shakespeare found names for the spirits Edgar says are tormenting Poor Tom (*King Lear*, III.vi).

Numerous and varied descriptions of witches were available to Shakespeare. Many, in pamphlets and in comedies and domestic dramas, were not appropriate for *Macbeth* as they were for Falstaff, in disguise as the fat woman of Brainford, when he is called 'you witch, you rag, you baggage, you polecat, you ronnion' (*Merry Wives of Windsor*, IV.ii.171–2). The possibility that the Witches in the play were no more threatening than this lies behind Banquo's questions on first encountering them, even though they 'look not like the inhabitants o' the earth' (I.iii.40). The familiar spirits who call to them at the start of the play, some of the ingredients of their cauldron, and the killing of swine, are reminiscent of the tales told of small-town and village witches. But Macbeth's initial silence and his following, 'Speak if you can,' show him to be more awed than his companion by their alien presence. Their 'withered' appearance may be reminiscent of the awesome witch in John Marston's *Tragedy of Sophonisba*, first staged in late spring 1605, just before the probable date for *Macbeth*, and itself indebted to Lucan's *Pharsalia*. She is said to have 'long unkempt hair' and:

> A loathsome yellow leanness spreads her face;
> A heavy hell-like paleness loads her cheeks.

Ben Jonson's *Masque of Queens*, performed at Court on 2 February 1609, was too late to influence the first version of *Macbeth* but illustrates theatrical possibilities that could derive from the range of classical texts that the published version gives as authority: writers including Apulieius, Cornelius Aggrippa, Homer, Horace, Lucan, Ovid, and Paracelsus among the better known. Jonson's twelve witches are governed by a 'Dame', not by Hecat, but they enter from Hell to 'a confused noise, with strange gestures'. In the printed text, Jonson notes that he had 'prescribed them their properties of vipers, snakes, bones, herbs, roots, and other ensigns of their magic, out of the authority of ancient and late writers'. Each brings an ingredient for their charm, for example:

> I have been gathering wolves' hairs,
> The mad dog's foam, and the adder's eares;
> The spurging [*discharge*] of a dead man's eyes,
> And all, since the evening star did rise.

Another 'kill'd an infant, to have his fat'. At their meetings they:

> do all things contrary to the custom of men, dancing, back to back, hip to hip, their hands join'd and making their circles backward, to the left hand, with strange fantastic motions of their heads, and bodies.

When their Dame joins them, she is 'naked arm'd, bare-footed, her frock tuck'd, her hair knotted and folded with vipers; in her hand, a torch made of a dead man's arm, lighted, girded with a snake'. She speaks in a peremptory manner, like Hecat in *Macbeth*:

> Well done, my hags. And come we, fraught with spight,
> To overthrow the glory of this night?
> Holds our great purpose?

In later classical literature, Hecate belongs to the underworld: for example, the poison administered by a player in *Hamlet* has been 'thrice blasted, thrice infected' with Hecate's curse (III.ii.246). Thomas Middleton's *The Witch*, which provided songs for the 1623 text of *Macbeth*, is a still cruder version of the same classically inspired theatrical spectacle (see the quotations at pp. 57 and 63). Both these works show the kind of creatures Shakespeare could have had in mind although nothing in either could have given him the slow fulfilment of prophecies and Macbeth's response to them: these features were unique to *Macbeth* in its time.

## Occasional sources and wider influences

Shakespeare's own earlier plays are the source of much in this tragedy. Echoes are everywhere: Richard the Third, like Macbeth, is a 'hell-hound'; both murderers imagine themselves wading through blood; both have terrible dreams and are deserted by their followers. Like Henry the Fourth, Macbeth cannot sleep: Henry asks, 'O sleep, O gentle sleep. / Nature's soft nurse, how have I frighted thee . . . ?' (2, *Henry IV*, III.i.5–6) and Macbeth knows that he 'does murder sleep . . . / Balm of hurt minds, great nature's second course, / Chief nourisher in life's feast' (II.ii.35–43). When an army marches against Macbeth, 'To give obedience where 'tis truly owed . . . / To dew the sovereign flower and drown the weeds,' issues from the earlier history plays are given compact and strongly placed expression. The close focus on Macbeth's and Lady Macbeth's inner consciousness depends on the broken syntax, varying rhythms, subtextual pressures, associative imagery, and the occasional accents of instinctive impulse that had been developed and mastered in earlier tragedies.

Shakespeare also drew upon his previous reading but in ways that make identification far from certain. Seneca's *Medea*, *Agamemnon*, *Hippolytus* and *Hercules Furens* may well have been recollected or studied afresh in English translations for Lady Macbeth's willingness to sacrifice a child and, more generally, for Macbeth's increasingly violent fear and remorse after his crime. Verbal parallels are not precise; if these plays were sources, they suggested ideas, images, and trains of thought and association rather than the phrasing of

speeches. For example, the bloodied hands of Lady Macbeth might
have derived from Medea's:

> How wilt thou from thy spouse depart? As him thou followed, haste
> In blood to bathe thy bloody hands and trait'rous lives to waste.

The influence of the Bible and Book of Common Prayer is far
more obvious and not always in specifically Christian contexts.
Psalm 90's 'we bring our years to an end, as it were a tale that is told'
may lie behind Macbeth's calling life a 'tale / Told by an idiot'
(V.v.26–7), and other phrases used in the Prayer Book's burial service
occur in the same soliloquy: 'Man . . . hath but a short time to live . . .
he fleeth as it were a shadow,' and 'earth to earth, ashes to ashes, dust
to death'. The injunction forbidding theatres to deal with matters of
religion may well be the reason why many references to Christian
thought and practice are imprecise or verbally changed, for example:
'In the great hand of God I stand' – 'The great doom's image' – 'God's
benison go with you' – 'Hell is murky' – 'The devil damn thee black' –
and, at the end, the 'juggling fiends', rather than the weird sisters or
witches, that 'palter with us in a double sense' (V.iv.58–61). All the
text's frequent references to damnation, blessedness, innocence and
eternity come from this huge, resonant, and deeply assimilated
source. In a society less obsessed with religion and less guided by its
practices than Shakespeare's England, we are likely to miss the original thrust and consequences of these obscured references, appreciat-
ing only their wider, less specific implications.

When the drunken Porter welcomes newcomers to Macbeth's
castle, Christian notions of damnation are undeniably present in a
protectively grotesque and laughable way. While summoning up
contemporary figures and recalling the court judgement on Father
Garnet, he sees himself among the devils at Hell's Gate as they had
been shown in the Miracle Plays that were performed until forbidden in the decades following the Reformation. In the Guild Chapel
that stands next to the Grammar School in Stratford-upon-Avon, a
fresco showed devils forcibly conducting the damned into hell.
Many preachers at church services would speak vividly about the
flames of hell, 'the everlasting bonfire' as the Porter calls them. Yet as

he imagines himself at the entrance to hell, this blear-eyed attendant also performs a role similar to St Peter's when he ushered souls to acceptance at the gates of heaven, another traditional function that Shakespeare had earlier invoked in *Much Ado About Nothing* (II.i.36–41). As the play's story moves towards murder, Shakespeare introduced a comedy performer and, in doing so, was able to draw on Christian beliefs and superstitions more specifically than elsewhere. The tragedy's original audiences were unlikely to underestimate the consequences of Macbeth's intended crime in the eyes of their God.

## The principal source

From Holinshed's *Chronicles* Shakespeare took the story of Donwald, who murdered King Duff, and combined it with that of Macbeth, who murdered Duncan. He stayed close to the wording of the second edition of 1587 for Macbeth's first meeting with the Witches and Malcolm's testing of Macduff in England but elsewhere freely modified what he read so that the re-working offers many insights into his creative purposes (see the Commentary, especially at pp. 14, 18–20, 71, 89, below). The addition of episodes not found at all in this source are especially suggestive: for example, the Witches' incantations and rituals (in I.i and ii, and in IV.i), the Porter's attendance at the castle's gate, the appearance of Banquo's ghost at the banquet, and Lady Macbeth's sleepwalking and reported suicide. Numerous small verbal echoes where the play is very different from the *Chronicles* show that Shakespeare had studied this source carefully before changing it to suit his own purposes.

Lengthy extracts are reprinted here to provide an approach to the play that is close to Shakespeare's own and can therefore reveal many of the choices he made and suggest some of his underlying intentions. Proper nouns are given in their most consistent original forms but all other spellings have been modernized. Punctuation has been altered as an aid to more fluent reading.

[Donwald] conceived such an inward malice towards the king (though he showed it not outward at the first) that the same continued still boiling in his stomach and ceased not till, through setting on of his wife and in revenge of such unthankfulness, he found means to murder the king within the foresaid castle of Fores where he used to sojourn. For the king being in that country, was accustomed to lie most commonly within the same castle, having a special trust in Donwald, as a man whom he never suspected.

But Donwald, not forgetting the reproach which his lineage had sustained by the execution of those his kinsmen whom the king for a spectacle to the people had caused to be hanged, could not but show manifest tokens of great grief at home amongst his family: which his wife perceiving, ceased not to travel with [*work upon*] him, till she understood what the cause was of his displeasure. Which at length when she had learned by his own relation, she as one that bare no less malice in her heart towards the king, for the like cause on her behalf than her husband did for his friends, counselled him (sith the king oftentimes used to lodge in his house without any guard about him, other than the garrison of the castle which was wholly at his commandment) to make him away, and showed him the means whereby he might soonest accomplish it.

Donwald, thus being the more kindled in wrath by the words of his wife, determined to follow her advice in the execution of so heinous an act. Whereupon devising with himself for a while which way he might best accomplish his cursed intent, at length he got opportunity, and sped his purpose as followeth. It chanced that the king upon the day before he purposed to depart forth of the castle, was long in his oratory at his prayers, and there continued till it was late in the night. At the last, coming forth, he called such afore him as had faithfully served him in pursuit and apprehension of the rebels, and giving them hearty thanks, he bestowed sundry honourable gifts amongst them, of the which number Donwald was one, as he that had been ever accounted a most faithful servant to the king.

At length, having talked with them a long time, he got him into his privy chamber, only with two of his chamberlains who, having brought him to bed, came forth again and then fell to banqueting with Donwald and his wife, who had prepared diverse delicate dishes and sundry sorts of drinks for their rear [*late*] supper or collation, whereat they sat up so long, till they had charged their stomachs with such full gorges that their heads where no sooner got to the pillow but asleep they were so fast that a man might have removed the chamber over them, sooner than to have awaked them out of their drunken sleep.

Then Donwald, though he abhorred the act greatly in heart, yet through instigation of his wife, he culled four of his servants unto him (whom he had made privy to his wicked intent before and framed to his purpose with large gifts) and now declaring unto them after what sort they should work the feat, they gladly obeyed his instructions &, speedily going about the murder, they enter the chamber (in which the king lay) a little before cock's crow, where they secretly cut his throat as he lay sleeping, without any buskling [*commotion*] at all: and immediately by a postern gate they carried forth the dead body into the fields and, throwing it upon an horse there provided ready for that purpose, they convey it unto a place, about two miles distant from the castle. . . . This they did by order appointed them by Donwald as is reported, for that the body should not be found, & by bleeding (when Donwald should be present) declare him to be guilty of the murder. For such an opinion men have, that the dead corpse of any man being slain, will bleed abundantly if the murderer be present. . . .

Donwald, about the time that the murder was in doing, got him amongst them that kept the watch, and so continued in the company with them all the residue of the night. But in the morning when the noise was raised in the king's chamber how the king was slain, his body conveyed away and the bed all berayed [*befouled*] with blood, he with the watch ran thither, as though he had known nothing of the matter, and breaking into the chamber, and finding cakes of blood in the bed and on the floor about the sides of it, he forthwith slew the chamberlains, as guilty of that heinous murder; and then like a mad man running to and fro, he ransacked every corner within the castle, as though it had been to have seen if he might have found either the body or any of the murderers hid in any privy place. But at length coming to the postern gate and finding it open, he burdened the chamberlains, whom he had slain, with all the fault, they having the keys of the gates committed to their keeping all the night, and therefore it could not be otherwise (said he) but that they were of counsel in the committing of that most detestable murder.

Finally, such was his over-earnest diligence in the severe inquisition and trial of the offenders herein, that some of the lords began to mislike the matter, and to smell forth shrewd tokens that he should not be altogether clear himself. But for so much as they were in that country where he had the whole rule, what by reason of his friends and authority together, they doubted [*were afraid*] to utter what they thought, till time and place should better serve thereunto, and hereupon got them away every man to his home. For the space of six months together, after this heinous murder thus committed, there appeared no sun by day, nor moon by night, in any part of the realm but still was the sky covered with continual clouds, and sometimes such outrageous winds arose, with lightnings and tempests, that the people were in great fear of present destruction. . . .

Monstrous sights also that were seen within the Scottish kingdom that year were these: horses in Louthian, being of singular beauty and swiftness, did eat their own flesh, and would in no wise taste any other meat. . . . There was a spar [*sparrowhawk*] also strangled by an owl. Neither was it any less wonder that the sun, as before is said, was continually covered with clouds for six months' space. But all men understood that the abominable murder of King Duffe was the cause hereof. . . .

*          *          *

[King Kenneth] might seem happy to all men . . . yet to himself he seemed most unhappy as he that could not but still live in continual fear, lest his wicked practice concerning the death of Malcolme Duffe should come to light and knowledge of the world. For so cometh it to pass that such as are pricked in conscience for any secret offence committed have ever an unquiet mind. And (as the fame goeth) it chanced that a voice was heard, as he was in bed in the night time to take his rest, uttering unto him these or the like words in effect: 'Think not Kenneth that the wicked slaughter of Malcolme Duffe, by thee contrived, is kept secret from the knowledge of the eternal God: thou art he that didst conspire the innocent's death. . . . It shall therefore come to pass that both thyself and thy issue, through the just vengeance of almighty God, shall suffer worthy punishment, to the infamy of thy house and family for evermore. . . .'

The king, with this voice being stricken into great dread and terror, passed that night without any sleep coming to his eyes.

*        *        *

Doada [daughter of King Malcolme] was married unto Sinell the Thane of Glammis, by whom she had issue, one Makbeth, a valiant gentleman and one that if he had not been somewhat cruel of nature, might have been thought most worthy the government of a realm. On the other part, Duncane [son of Malcolme's other daughter, who had succeeded him as king] was so soft and gentle of nature that the people wished the inclinations and manners of these two cousins to have been so tempered and interchangeably bestowed between them that, where the one had too much of clemency and the other of cruelty, the mean virtue betwixt these two extremities might have reigned by indifferent partition in them both: so should Duncane have proved a worthy king, and Makbeth an excellent captain. The beginning of Duncane's reign was very quiet and peaceable, without any notable trouble; but after it was perceived how negligent he was in punishing offenders, many misruled persons took occasion thereof to trouble the peace and quiet state of the commonwealth, by seditious commotions which first had their beginnings in this wise.

Banquho, the Thane of Lochquhaber, of whom the house of the Stewards is descended, the which by order of lineage hath now for a long time enjoyed the crown of Scotland, even till these our days, as he gathered the finances due to the king, and further punished somewhat sharply such as were notorious offenders, being assailed by a number of rebels inhabiting in that country and spoiled of the money and all other things, had much ado to get away with life, after he had received sundry grievous wounds amongst them. Yet escaping their hands . . . he repaired to the court where, making his complaint to the king in most earnest wise, he purchased at length that the offenders were sent for by a Sergeant at Arms, to appear to make answer unto such matters as should be laid to their charge: but they augmenting their mischievous act with a more wicked deed, after they had misused the messenger with sundry kinds of reproaches, they finally slew him also.

Then doubting not but for such contemptuous demeanour

against the king's regal authority, they should be invaded with all
the power the king could make, Makdowald, one of great estima-
tion among them, making first a confederacy with his nearest
friends and kinsmen, took upon him to be chief captain of all such
rebels as would stand against the king, in maintenance of their
grievous offences lately committed against him. Many slander-
ous words also, and railing taunts, this Makdowald uttered
against his prince, calling him a faint-hearted milksop, more meet
to govern a sort of idle monks in some cloister than to have the
rule of such valiant and hardy men of war as the Scots were. He
used also such subtle persuasions and forged allurements that in
small time he had gotten together a mighty power of men; for out
of the western Isles there came unto him a great multitude of
people, offering themselves to assist him in that rebellious quarrel, and out of Ireland in hope of the spoil came no small number
of Kerns and Galloglasses. . . .

At length Makbeth, speaking much against the king's softness
and overmuch slackness in punishing offenders, whereby they
had such time to assemble together, he promised, notwithstanding, if the charge were committed unto him and unto Banquho,
so to order the matter that the rebels should be shortly
vanquished and quite put down, and that not so much as one of
them should be found to make resistance within the country.

And even so it came to pass. . . . Thus was justice and law
restored again to the old accustomed course by the diligent
means of Makbeth. Immediately whereupon word came that
Sueno, King of Norway, was arrived in Fife with a puissant army,
to subdue the whole realm of Scotland. . . . [After several encounters with varying fortunes,] word was brought that a new fleet of
Danes was arrived at Kingcorn, sent thither by Canute, King of
England, in revenge of his brother Sueno's overthrow. To resist
these enemies, which were already landed and busy in spoiling
the country, Makbeth and Banquho were sent with the king's
authority, who having with them a convenient power, encountered the enemies, slew part of them, and chased the other to
their ships. They that escaped and got once to their ships,
obtained of Makbeth, for a great sum of gold, that such of their
friends as were slain at this last bickering, might be buried in
Saint Colme's Inch. . . .

And these were the wars that Duncane had with foreign

enemies, in the seventh year of his reign. Shortly after happened a strange and uncouth wonder, which afterward was the cause of much trouble in the realm of Scotland, as ye shall after hear. It fortuned as Makbeth and Banquho journeyed towards Fores where the king then lay, they went sporting by the way together without other company, save only themselves, passing through the woods and fields, when suddenly in the midst of [open] land, there met them three women in strange and wild apparel, resembling creatures of elder world, whom when they attentively beheld, wondering much at the sight, the first of them spake and said: 'All hail Macbeth, Thane of Glammis' (for he had lately entered into that dignity and office by the death of his father Sinell). The second of them said: 'Hail Makbeth, Thane of Cawder.' But the third said: 'All hail Makbeth, that hereafter shalt be King of Scotland.'

Then Banquho: 'What manner of women', saith he, 'are you, that seem so little favourable unto me, whereas to my fellow here, besides high offices, ye assign also the kingdom, appointing forth nothing for me at all?' 'Yes,' saith the first of them, 'we promise greater benefits unto thee, than unto him, for he shall reign in deed, but with an unlucky end; neither shall he leave any issue behind him to succeed in his place, where contrarily thou shalt in deed not reign at all, but of thee those shall be born which shall govern the Scottish kingdom by long order of continual descent.' Herewith the foresaid women vanished immediately out of their sight. This was reputed at the first but some vain fantastical illusion by Makbeth and Banquho, insomuch that Banquho would call Makbeth in jest, King of Scotland; and Makbeth again would call him in sport likewise, the father of many kings. But afterwards the common opinion was, that these women were either the weird sisters, that is (as ye would say) the goddesses of destiny, or else some nymphs or fairies, endued with knowledge of prophecy by their necromantical science, because everything came to pass as they had spoken. For shortly after, the Thane of Cawder being condemned at Fores of treason against the king committed, his lands, livings, and offices were given of the king's liberality to Makbeth.

The same night after, at supper, Banquho jested with him and said, 'Now Makbeth thou hast obtained those things which the two former sisters prophesied, there remaineth only for thee to

purchase that which the third said should come to pass.'
Whereupon Makbeth, revolving the thing in his mind, began
even then to devise how he might attain to the kingdom; but yet
he thought with himself that he must tarry a time, which should
advance him thereto (by the divine providence) as it had come to
pass in his former preferment. But shortly after it chanced that
King Duncane, having two sons by his wife which was the daughter of Seyward, Earl of Northumberland, he made the elder of
them called Malcolme, Prince of Cumberland, as it were thereby
to appoint him his successor in the kingdom, immediately after
his decease. Makbeth sore troubled herewith, for that he saw by
this means his hope sore hindered (where, by the old laws of the
realm, the ordinance was that, if he that should succeed were not
of able age to take the charge upon himself, he that was next of
blood unto him should be admitted) he began to take counsel
how he might usurp the kingdom by force, having a just quarrel
so to do (as he took the matter) for that Duncane did what in him
lay to defraud him of all manner of title and claim which he
might, in time to come, pretend unto the crown.

The words of the three weird sisters also . . . greatly encouraged him hereunto, but specially his wife lay sore upon him to
attempt the thing, as she that was very ambitious, burning in
unquenchable desire to bear the name of a queen. At length
therefore, communicating his purposed intent with his trusty
friends, amongst whom Banquho was the chiefest, upon confidence of their promised aid, he slew the king at Enverns, or (as
some say) at Botgosuane, in the sixth year of his reign. Then
having a company about him of such as he had made privy to his
enterprise, he caused himself to be proclaimed king, and forthwith went unto Scone, where (by common consent) he received
the investure of the kingdom according to the accustomed
manner. The body of Duncane was first conveyed unto Elgine, &
there buried in kingly wise; but afterwards it was removed and
conveyed unto Colmekill, and there laid in a sepulcher amongst
his predecessors, in the year after the birth of our Saviour, 1046.

Malcolme Cammore and Donald Bane, the sons of King
Duncane, for fear of their lives (which they might well know that
Makbeth would seek to bring to an end for his more sure confirma-
tion in the estate) fled into Cumberland, where Malcolme remained,
till time that Saint Edward, the son of Etheldred, recovered the

dominion of England from the Danish power, the which Edward received Malcolme by way of most friendly entertainment; but Donald passed over into Ireland, where he was tenderly cherished by the king of that land. Makbeth, after the departure thus of Duncane's sons, used great liberality towards the nobles of the realm, thereby to win their favour; and when he saw that no man went about to trouble him, he set his whole intention to maintain justice and to punish all enormities and abuses which had chanced through the feeble and slothful administration of Duncane. . . . He made many wholesome laws and statutes for the public weal of his subjects. . . .

These and the like commendable laws Makbeth caused to be put as then in use, governing the realm for the space of ten years in equal [*impartial*] justice. But this was but a counterfeit zeal of equity showed by him, partly against his natural inclination, to purchase thereby the favour of the people. Shortly after, he began to show what he was, instead of equity, practising cruelty. For the prick of conscience (as it chanceth ever in tyrants and such as attain to any estate by unrighteous means) caused him ever to fear, lest he should be served of the same cup as he had ministered to his predecessor. The words also of the three weird sisters would not out of his mind, which as they promised him the kingdom, so likewise did they promise it at the same time unto the posterity of Banquho. He willed therefore the same Banquho, with his son named Fleance, to come to a supper that he had prepared for them, which was in deed, as he had devised, present death at the hands of certain murderers, whom he hired to execute that deed, appointing them to meet with the same Banquho and his son without the palace, as they returned to their lodgings, and there to slay them, so that he would not have his house slandered, but that in time to come he might clear himself, if any thing were laid to his charge upon any suspicion that might arise.

It chanced yet by the benefit of the dark night, that though the father were slain, the son yet by the help of Almighty God reserving him to better fortune, escaped that danger. . . .

After the contrived slaughter of Banquho, nothing prospered with the foresaid Makbeth; for in manner every man began to doubt his own life, and durst unneth [*without need, was afraid to*] appear in the king's presence; and even as there were many that stood in fear of him, so likewise stood he in fear of many, in such sort that he began to make those away, by one surmised cavilation [*spurious reason*] or other, whom he thought most able to work him any displeasure.

At length he found such sweetness by putting his nobles thus to death, that his earnest thirst after blood in this behalf might in no wise be satisfied, for ye must consider he won double profit (as he thought) hereby: for first, they were rid out of the way whom he feared, and then again his coffers were enriched by their goods which were forfeited to his use, whereby he might the better maintain a guard of armed men about him to defend his person from injury of them whom he had in any suspicion. Further, to the end he might the more cruelly oppress his subjects with all tyrant-like wrongs, he built a strong castle on the top of a hill called Dunsinane, situate in Gowrie, ten miles from Perth, on such a proud height that, standing there aloft, a man might behold well near all the countries of Angus, Fife, Stermond, and Ernedale, as it were lying underneath him. This castle, then being founded on the top of that high hill, put the realm to great charges before it was finished, for all the stuff necessary to the building could not be brought up without much toil and business. But Makbeth, being once determined to have the work go forward, caused the thanes of each shire within the realm to come and help towards that building, each man his course about.

At the last, when the turn fell unto Makduffe, Thane of Fife, to build his part, he sent workmen with all needful provision, and commanded them to show such diligence in every behalf that no occasion might be given for the king to find fault with him, in that he came not himself as other had done, which he refused to do, for doubt lest the king, bearing him . . . no great good will, could lay violent hands upon him. . . . Shortly after, Makbeth coming to behold how the work went forward, and because he found not Makduffe there, he was sore offended, and said: 'I perceive this man will never obey my commandments till he be ridden with a snaffle: but I shall provide well enough for him. . . .' Neither could he afterwards abide to look upon the said Makduffe, either for that he thought his puissance over great; either else for that he had learned of certain wizards, in whose words he put great confidence (for that the prophecy had happened so right which the three fairies or weird sisters had declared unto him) how that he ought to take heed of Makduffe, who in time to come should seek to destroy him.

And surely hereupon had he put Makduffe to death, but that a certain witch, whom he had in great trust, had told that he should never be slain with man born of any woman, nor vanquished till the wood of Bernane came to the castle of Dunsinane. By this prophecy Makbeth put all fear out of his heart, supposing he might do what he would, without any fear to be punished for the same, for by the one prophecy he believed it was unpossible for any man to vanquish him, and by the other unpossible to slay him. This vain hope caused him to do many outrageous things, to the grievous oppression of his subjects. At length Makduffe, to avoid peril of life, purposed with himself to pass into England, to procure Malcolme Cammore to claim the crown of Scotland. But this was not so secretly devised by Makduffe but that Macbeth had knowledge given him thereof; for kings (as is said) have sharp sight like unto lynx, and long ears like unto Midas. For Makbeth had in every nobleman's house one sly fellow or other in fee with him, to reveal all that was said or done within the same, by which slight he oppressed the most part of the nobles of his realm.

Immediately then, being advertised whereabout Makduffe went, he came hastily with a great power into Fife, and forthwith besieged the castle where Makduffe dwelled, trusting to have found him therein. They that kept the house, without any resistance opened the gates and suffered him to enter, mistrusting none evil. But nevertheless Makbeth most cruelly caused the wife and children of Makduffe, with all other whom he found in that castle, to be slain. Also he confiscated the goods of Makduffe, proclaimed him traitor, and confined him out of all the parts of his realm; but Makduffe was already escaped out of danger, and gotten into England unto Malcolme Cammore, to try what purchase he might make by means of his support to revenge the slaughter so cruelly executed on his wife, his children, and other friends. At his coming unto Malcolme, he declared into what great misery the estate of Scotland was brought by the detestable cruelties exercised by the tyrant Makbeth, having committed many horrible slaughters and murders, both as well of the nobles as commons, for the which he was hated right mortally of all his liege people, desiring nothing more than to be delivered of that intolerable and most heavy yoke of thralldom, which they sustained at such a caitiff's hands.

Malcolme hearing Makduffe's words, which he uttered in very lamentable sort, for mere compassion and very ruth that pierced his sorrowful heart, bewailing the miserable state of his country, he fetched a deep sigh; which Makduffe perceiving, began to fall most earnestly in hand with him to enterprise the delivering of the Scottish people out of the hands of so cruel and bloody a tyrant, as Makbeth by too many plain experiments did show himself to be: which was an easy matter for him to bring to pass, considering not only the good title he had, but also the earnest desire of the people to have some occasion ministered whereby they might be revenged of those notable injuries, which they daily sustained by the outrageous cruelty of Makbeth's misgovernance. Though Malcolme was very sorrowful for the oppression of his countrymen the Scots, in manner as Makduffe had declared; yet doubting whether he were come as one that meant unfeignedly as he spake, or else as sent from Makbeth to betray him, he thought to have some further trial, and thereupon, dissembling his mind at the first, he answered as followeth: 'I am truly very sorry for the misery chanced to my country of Scotland but, though I have never so great affection to relieve the same, yet by reason of certain incurable vices which reign in me, I am nothing meet thereto. First, such immoderate lust and voluptuous sensuality (the abominable fountain of all vices) followeth me that, if I were made king of Scots, I should seek to deflower your maids and matrons, in such wise that mine intemperancy should be more importable unto you than the bloody tyranny of Makbeth now is.'

Hereunto Makduffe answered: 'This surely is a very evil fault, for many noble princes and kings have lost both lives and kingdoms for the same; nevertheless there are women enough in Scotland and therefore follow my counsel: make thyself king, and I shall convey the matter so wisely that thou shalt be so satisfied at thy pleasure in such secret wise, that no man shall be aware thereof.'

Then said Malcolme: 'I am also the most avaricious creature on the earth, so that if I were king I should seek so many ways to get lands and goods that I would slay the most part of all the nobles of Scotland by surmised accusations, to the end I might enjoy their lands, goods, and possessions. ... Suffer me to remain where I am, lest if I attain to the regiment of your realm, mine unquenchable avarice may prove such that ye would think the displeasures which now grieve you should seem easy in respect of the unmeasurable outrage which might ensue through my coming amongst you.'

Makduffe to this made answer, how it was a far worse fault than the other: 'For avarice is the root of all mischief, and for that crime the most part of our kings have been slain and brought to their final end, yet, notwithstanding, follow my counsel, and take upon thee the crown. There is gold and riches enough in Scotland to satisfy thy greedy desire.' Then said Malcolme again, 'I am furthermore inclined to dissimulation, telling of leasings and all other kinds of deceit, so that I naturally rejoice in nothing so much as to betray & deceive such as put any trust or confidence in my words. Then, sith there is nothing that more becometh a prince than constancy, verity, truth, and justice, with the other laudable fellowship of those fair and noble virtues which are comprehended only in soothfastness, and that lying utterly overthroweth the same, you see how unable I am to govern any province or region: and therefore, sith you have remedies to cloak and hide all the rest of my other vices, I pray you find shift to cloak this vice amongst the residue.'

Then said Makduffe: 'This is yet the worst of all, and there I leave thee, and therefore say: O ye unhappy and miserable Scottishmen, which are thus scourged with so many and sundry calamities, each one above the other! Ye have one cursed and wicked tyrant that now reigneth over you, without any right or title, oppressing you with his most bloody cruelty. This other that hath the right to the crown, is so replete with the inconstant behaviour and manifest vices of Englishmen that he is nothing worthy to enjoy it. ... Adieu Scotland! for now I account myself a banished man for ever, without comfort or consolation'; and with those words, the brackish tears trickled down his cheeks very abundantly.

At the last, when he was ready to depart, Malcolme took him by the sleeve, and said: 'Be of good comfort, Makduffe, for I have none of these vices before remembered, but have jested with thee in this manner, only to prove thy mind: for diverse times heretofore hath Makbeth sought by this manner of means to bring me into his hands. But the more slow I have showed myself to condescend to thy motion and request, the more diligence shall I use in accomplishing the same.' Incontinently hereupon, they embraced each other and, promising to be faithful the one to the other, they fell in consultation how they might best provide for all their business, to bring the same to good effect. . . .

Malcolme purchased such favour at King Edward's hands that old Siward, Earl of Northumberland, was appointed with ten thousand men to go with him into Scotland, to support him in this enterprise for recovery of his right. After these news were spread abroad in Scotland, the nobles drew into two several factions, the one taking part with Makbeth and the other with Malcolme. . . . After that Makbeth perceived his enemies' power to increase, by such aid as came to them forth of England with his adversary Malcolme, he recoiled back into Fife, there purposing to abide in camp fortified, at the castle of Dunsisnane, and to fight with his enemies, if they meant to pursue him. . . . His own subjects . . . stole daily from him but he had such confidence in his prophecies that he believed he should never be vanquished till Birnane wood were brought to Dunsinane; nor yet to be slain with any man that should be or was born of any woman.

Malcolme, following hastily after Makbeth, came the night before the battle unto Birnane wood, and when his army had rested for a while there to refresh them, he commanded every man to get a bough of some tree or other of that wood in his hand, as big as he might bear, and to march forth therewith in such wise that, on the next morrow, they might come closely [*secretly*] and without sight in this manner within view of his enemies. On the morrow when Makbeth beheld them coming in this sort, he first marvelled what the matter meant, but in the end remembered himself that the prophecy, which he had heard long before that time, of the coming of Birnane wood to Dunsinane castle, was likely to be now fulfilled. Nevertheless, he brought his men in order of battle, and exhorted them to do valiantly. Howbeit his enemies had scarcely cast from them their boughs, when Makbeth perceiving their numbers, betook him straight to flight, whom Makduffe pursued with great hatred even till he came unto Lunfannaine, where Makbeth perceiving that Makduffe was hard at his back, leapt beside his horse, saying:

'Thou traitor, what meaneth it that thou shouldest thus in vain follow me that am not appointed to be slain by any creature that is born of a woman? Come on therefore, and receive thy reward which thou deserved for thy pains!' – and therewithal he lift up his sword thinking to have slain him.

But Makduffe, quickly avoiding from his horse ere he came at him, answered (with his naked sword in his hand) saying: 'It is true Makbeth, and now shall thine insatiable cruelty have an end, for I am even he that thy wizards have told thee of, who was never born of my mother, but ripped out of her womb.' Therewithal, he stepped unto him, and slew him in the place. Then cutting his head from his shoulders, he set it upon a pole, and brought it unto Malcolme. This was the end of Makbeth, after he had reigned 17 years over the Scottishmen. In the beginning of his reign he accomplished many worthy acts, very profitable to the commonwealth (as ye have heard), but afterward by illusion of the devil, he defamed the same with most terrible cruelty. He was slain in the year of the incarnation 1057, and in the 16 year of King Edward's reign over the Englishmen.

Malcolme Cammore thus recovering the realm ... was crowned at Scone the 25 day of April, in the year of our Lord 1057. Immediately after his coronation he called a parliament at Forfair, in the which he rewarded them with lands and livings that had assisted him against Makbeth, advancing them to fees and offices as he saw cause, & commanded that specially those that bare the surname of any offices or lands should have and enjoy the same. He created many earls, lords, barons, and knights. Many of them that before were thanes, were at this time made earls, as Fife, Menteth, Atholl, Levenox, Murrey, Cathnes, Rosse, and Angus. These were the first earls that have been heard of amongst the Scottishmen (as their histories do make mention).

\*     \*     \*

[In the battle] in which Earl Siward vanquished the Scots, one of Siward's sons chanced to be slain, whereof although the father had good cause to be sorrowful, yet, when he heard that he died of a wound which he had received in fighting stoutly, in the forepart of his body, and that with his face towards the enemy, he greatly rejoiced thereat, to hear that he died so manfully. . . . When his father heard the news, he demanded whether he received the wound whereof he died, in the forepart of the body or in the hinder part; and when it was told him that he received it in the forepart: 'I rejoice,' saith he, 'even with all my heart, for I would not wish either to my son nor to myself any other kind of death.'

*       *       *

In diet and apparel [Edward the Confessor, King of England] was spare and nothing sumptuous: and although on high feasts he wore rich apparel, as became the majesty of his royal personage, yet he showed no proud nor lofty countenance, rather praising God for his bountiful goodness towards him extended, than esteeming herein the vain pomp of the world. . . . As hath been thought, he was inspired with the gift of prophecy, and also to have had the gift of healing infirmities and diseases. He used to help those that were vexed with the disease, commonly called the king's evil, and left that virtue as it were a portion of inheritance unto his successors, the kings of this realm.

# 4 Key Productions and Performances

The commentary in this book has concentrated on what the text of *Macbeth* asks actors to do and how it can work in their minds and imaginations. This is the heart of any staging of the play: from this core is derived the shape and timing of a production and the life that actors give to every detail of performance. The unspoken text is the one more or less constant element in every production but to understand what it becomes in any one performance much more has to be considered. The commentary has repeatedly shown how the life given to words in performance depends on the choices and instincts of the principal actors and on the personal qualities of each highly individual presence on stage: all this makes every performance unique and extremely difficult to describe once it is complete and becomes a thing of the past. Besides the text and actors, a production is always influenced by the shape, size, and technical equipment of the stage, and the shape, size, and location of the theatre: the commentary has been able to give little attention to these factors. And it has given none at all to the exact date of a performance, its cultural and political context, or the composition and mood of its audience. All these factors have considerable effect on how the play has been and will be performed at any one time, and their interaction makes the study of productions and performances – of a play so challenging as *Macbeth* – a fascinating subject for advanced research and criticism. Its history in performance is a still more complicated subject that has been the subject of numerous books.

For readers making a first or renewed approach to understanding what this play can become in production, the most rewarding way is to study a small number of contrasted performances within a broadly sketched historical outline. Four performances will be discussed in sufficient detail to give some sense of their overall shape and impact, as well as noting some examples of the actors' handling of the text. Reference will be made to a handful of other productions in order to illustrate the richness and variety of the play's history on stage. Armed with these examples, a reader should be ready to research other productions and consider any new performances with a clearer awareness of what has been achieved.

## Davenant, Garrick and Mrs Siddons

Little can be said of early performances because almost no evidence has survived. We do know that Richard Burbage played Macbeth and we may almost as safely assume that Robert Armin was the Porter. Burbage, a sharer in the actors' company and its most famous performer, was capable of parts at least as varied as Lear, Hamlet, and Othello. His range, therefore, could encompass both authority and child-like madness, keen intelligence and restless physicality, military decisiveness and passionate sexuality. Very few actors have had the opportunity to develop such diversity today with the flexibility to make it possible in a repertoire that changes daily, and yet the Commentary has shown how often and how variously the text draws upon such a breadth of talents. Armin, the company's leading and independently minded fool, had an idiosyncratic stage presence and was skilled in imitation and physical transformations. He was also renowned for improvised performances, being able as a solo performer to take up whatever topics were suggested to him. He tended not to interact with his audiences by playing directly to them, preferring to perform *for* them, while being responsive to their presence and topical interests. The commentary notes how the Porter's short role in Act II, scene iii, suits such a performer as a solo spot.

The staging of the play during the first centuries of its stage life showed a marked tendency to change the sequence of scenes, deleting and adding to the text and augmenting the impact of the witches with spectacle and music, in much the same way as the changes that were incorporated in the Folio text soon after the very first performances (see above, pp. 2–3). Two early promptbooks have survived, each with its own amendments and cuts, simplifying the images and syntax of the dialogue, deleting whole episodes and cast-members – the Porter, Macbeth's interview with the murderers, much of the 'England scene' (IV.iii). A version written by William Davenant (1606–68) for performance in his own theatre in the 1660s was published posthumously in 1674 and was a popular success, with Thomas Betterton (1635–1710) in the title role. The text by this playwright, who claimed to be the illegitimate son of Shakespeare, was to have a lasting influence on what audiences saw, some of its *divertissements* being further developed so that in the nineteenth century large numbers of witches would fly through the air accompanied by an orchestra.

Davenant's published text cuts the Apparitions of Act IV, scene i, keeping only shortened versions of their predictions, but the Witches fly through the air and have an extra scene in Act II so that they can appear to Macduff and Lady Macduff, singing, dancing, and foretelling what will happen. Hecat, who was to sing in a bass voice, has an enhanced role with songs and dialogue derived from Middleton's *The Witch*. Shakespeare's 'Weird sisters', at once awesome to Macbeth and Banquo, become a spectacular and singing chorus played by male actors with spoken dialogue that must often have been comic in effect. Elsewhere Shakespeare's dialogue is shortened and simplified to avoid what was considered too obscure and hard to understand. While verbally simple passages, like the exchanges between Lady Macbeth and her husband immediately after the murder, are retained, the soliloquies and longer speeches are reduced in length, imagery, intensity, verbal complexity, and syntactical subtlety. For lines that are now familiar and of crucial importance for any actor, Davenant provided:

> If it were well when done; then it were well
> It were done quickly; if his death might be
> Without the death of nature in my self,
> And killing my own rest; it wou'd suffice;
> But deeds of this complexion still return
> To plague the doer, and destroy his peace:
> Yet let me think; he's here in double trust. . . .

Revisions of the plot were equally thorough and, for us today, are a reminder of some basic problems that Shakespeare's text sets for every production that wishes to keep all that he wrote. Although the interrogation of the murderers and the England scene are retained in shortened and simplified form, the Porter is gone, the role of the Old Man in Act II, scene iv is one of many short appearances given to Seyton, and it is Lennox and not young Seyward who is killed by Macbeth. The most significant of these changes gave Macduff whole scenes and extra lines so that he becomes a reliable and heroic counterpart to Macbeth. After the discovery of Duncan's murder, he, and not Banquo, is fully and reasonably in charge:

> I find this place too public for true sorrow:
> Let us retire, and mourn: but first,
> Guarded by virtue, I'm resolv'd to find
> The utmost of this business.

At the end of the tragedy, Macbeth is left alone on stage to die, with a final line – 'Farewell vain World, and what's most vain in it, Ambition' – and Macduff, who re-enters to Malcolm and the assembled armies, bears his adversary's sword, not his severed head. He also has more to say, including:

>      . . . here I present you with
> The tyrant's sword, to show that Heaven appointed
> Me to take revenge for you, and all
> That suffered by his power.

When tastes changed in more sentimental and romantic times, spectacular elements from Davenant's version were retained while the Folio was progressively reinstated. David Garrick (1717–79), actor, theatre manager, and author, worked much like a modern director by reining in the Witches' comedy and relying more on Shakespeare's text. He had less respect for the play's plot and structure. For the ending, he followed Davenant in having Macduff leave the stage so that Macbeth dies alone; he then speaks lines that he had written himself to make the hero's sentiments explicit:

'Tis done! the scene of life will quickly close.
Ambition's vain, delusive dreams are fled,
And now I wake to darkness, guilt and horror;
I cannot bear it! Let me shake it off –
'Two' not be; my soul is clogg'd with blood –
I cannot rise! I dare not ask for mercy –
It is too late, hell drags me down; I sink,
I sink – Oh! – my soul is lost for ever!
Oh!

Nevertheless, Garrick's performance became legendary, especially for those moments of astonishment and feeling to which he brought a total physical commitment. From the very start, his Macbeth was motivated by ambition: it 'kindles at the distant prospect of a crown when the witches prophesy' it will be his. After the murder the text was spoken in 'terrifying whispers':

> You heard what they spoke, but you learned more from the agitation of mind displayed in their action and deportment . . . the dark colouring given by the actor to these abrupt speeches makes the scene awful and tremendous to the autditors.   (Bartholomeusz, pp. 41, 60)

While the fame of Garrick's Macbeth lasted long after his death, his performance becoming a standard by which others were judged, the achievement of Hannah Pritchard as his Lady was eclipsed by that of Sarah Siddons (1755–1831). After her first London appearance in the role in 1785 her performances were frequently described and her 'Remarks on the Character of Lady Macbeth', provided for her biographer a few years after her last performance in 1812, give her own view of the character. She wrote that she had visualized a person who was 'fair, feminine, nay, perhaps, even fragile' and yet had the energy and strength of mind to enthral her husband, 'a hero so dauntless, a character so amiable, so honourable as Macbeth'. Sarah Siddons had the imagination and expressive abilities to realize this clash of qualities when her 'vaulting ambition and intrepid daring' drive him to commit the terrible crimes from which he has instinctively recoiled. By Act III, with his confidence and her peace of mind gone, she must struggle to support his weakness. Reaching the Banquet scene (III.iv), her 'restless and terrifying glances towards her husband' would amaze their guests as much as her husband's helpless terror. Eyewitnesses report that for 'Glamis thou art, and Cawdor, and shalt be / What thou art promised' (I.v.13–14), she used an 'exalted prophetic tone, as if the whole future were present to her soul' and that 'the amazing burst of energy upon the words "shalt be" perfectly electrified the house'. In her sleepwalking, she 'moved her lips involuntarily; all her gestures were involuntary and mechanical. . . . She glided on and off the stage almost like an apparition' (Booth et al. 1996, pp. 40–5). Performing in this manner took a great deal of time and made difficulties for the actor who played opposite. Fortunately, in the later part of the thirty years when she played the role from time to time in repertory, the role of Macbeth was played by her brother, John Philip Kemble, who with an imposing and well-grounded presence was able to keep his own hold on the audience's attention.

Elizabeth Inchbald (1753–1821), an actress turned playwright and novelist, in an introduction to a published version of Kemble's acting version, gives an admiring account of the play in his well-equipped and well-managed theatre that can sum up its entertaining and uplifting reputation in this romantic age:

> The huge rocks, the enormous caverns, and blasted heaths of Scotland, in the scenery; – the highland warrior's dress, of centuries past, worn by soldiers and their generals; – the splendid robes and banquet at the royal court held at Fores; – the awful, yet inspiring music, which accompanies words assimilated to each sound; – and, above all – the fear, the terror, the remorse; – the agonizing throbs and throes, which speak in looks, whispers, sudden starts, and writhings, by Kemble and Mrs Siddons, all tending to one great precept – *Thou shalt not murder,* – render this play one of the most impressive moral lessons which the stage exhibits.

### Henry Irving and Ellen Terry

However spectacular the staging, *Macbeth* depends in performance on skilled and experienced actors with commanding stage presence, strong imagination, and courage. After Siddons and Garrick, Ellen Terry and Henry Irving, together, were to take the most compelling hold on the tragedy. His first appearance in the role at the Lyceum Theatre in London was under Mrs Bateman's management in 1875 but it was on 29 December 1888, under his own management at the same theatre, that he played opposite Ellen Terry and both established their claim to the roles. That they had already played together for ten years in numerous plays by Shakespeare and contemporary authors was a huge advantage and so was the long-running success of Irving's company at the Lyceum, which made possible the sustained study that each brought to their performances.

Theatre at this time was thriving and prosperous, as it had not been for centuries. In 1882, the *Daily News* had reported that Greater London had 57 licensed theatres and 415 music halls, with a combined nightly capacity of 302,000. Irving's Lyceum was notable among these for drawing to the theatre many who had 'formerly held aloof from it' (*The New Era*, May 1878): in his audiences were members of all classes, including the educated and ambitious middle class. Performances were appreciated and criticized in detail by numerous papers at a length that is not possible today. New productions were eagerly anticipated. Souvenir programmes and memorabilia were available. Irving was the first actor to be knighted.

The production of *Macbeth* came at the height of success for the two actors and had all the advantages of their practised and almost equal partnership. Both have left written accounts of their approach to the roles and their subsequent reflections on them. By means of these notes, articles and lectures, together with many reviews, eyewitness accounts, and drawings of performers and stage settings, research can piece together what happened in almost every scene and give a credible impression of the effect of the two main performances. The following account draws upon Alan Hughes's *Henry Irving, Shakespearean* (1981).

Irving created a thoughtful villain who felt no real pangs of conscience. Later, in an 'Address on the Character of Macbeth', he explained:

> He was a poet with his brain and a villain with his heart . . . he loved throughout to paint himself and his deeds in the blackest pigments and to bring to the exercise of his wickedness the conscious deliberation of an

intellectual voluptuary. . . . Macbeth – hypocrite, traitor, and regicide –
threw over his crimes the glamour of his own poetic self-torturing
thought . . . playing with conscience so that action and reaction of poetic
thought might send emotional waves through the brain while the resolution was as firmly fixed as steel and the heart as cold as ice . . . the man of
sensibility and not the man of feeling.    (Quoted in Hughes, p. 101)

Because it was not in her nature, Ellen Terry was, from the start,
very sure that she would not follow the same course as the ambitious
and assured Lady Macbeth of Mrs Siddons. Rather she would emphasize the love that made the wife supportive and solicitous of her
husband whatever he might do; she believed him worthy of the
crown, and not until after the murder did she realize that the crime
had destroyed both herself and him. When he told her 'We will
proceed no further in this business' (I.vii.31), she treated the change as
cowardice, which she must help him to overcome. She became
strong for his sake: when she told him that she would have 'dashed
the brains out' of her infant at her breast rather than go back on such
a decision, she was seen to brush away a tear, so hard was the effort.
While he sat dazed, she continued to speak 'slowly and charmingly,
kneeling beside him and playing with his hands'. After the murder,
when he could not say amen to the grooms' prayer, the actress noted
that 'Consider it not so deeply' (II.ii.30) should not be 'stern and
angry' but full of 'feminine consideration mixed with alarm' (Hughes,
pp. 103–4).

From the discovery of Duncan's murder onwards the two responsible for the crime grew ever further apart, each isolated and tortured
in mind and body. According to Irving's 'Account of the Character',
Macbeth's resolve that 'For mine own good, / All causes shall give
way' (III.iv.135–6) 'announces his fixed intent on a general career of
selfish crime': he is 'steeped so far' in blood that he cannot turn back.
'No need of his wife now', Irving wrote in a copy of the text; instead,
he turns to common cut-throats. When faced with Macduff, he can
only 'try the last' (V.vi.71). At this moment, 'Before my body / I throw
my warlike shield' was cut from the text because he had already
thrown it away. As Macbeth was progressively seen to be damned,
his wife was 'brought through agony and sin to repentance, and was

forgiven', as Ellen Terry told her biographer, and she had made notes to the same effect in a copy of the text. She played the final sleep-walking scene as aged and weak, in a plain white gown, swaying slightly as she walked, speaking in a 'long-drawn, almost whining' way. On 'Here's the smell of blood still' (V.i.48), Terry noted that she rubbed her hands together – 'trembling hands – she is *very* weak'.

The Lyceum *Macbeth* was also famed for its staging. Irving had the financial resources and the experienced staff to provide a sequence of lavish scenes and costumes, designed by well-known artists. The theatre had been equipped with electric lighting, its auditorium dark-ened, and its technicians had become capable of subtle and striking effects that astonished audiences. For *Macbeth*, music was written by Sir Arthur Sullivan and played by an orchestra. In his first scene, Macbeth was followed by a large army swarming across the stage against the background of a fiery sky. Duncan arrived at Macbeth's castle by moonlight across a giant sloping drawbridge between lines of attendants holding torches. Women bowed as Lady Macbeth came to greet him, accompanied by 'serene and beautiful music'. For the Apparition scene (IV.i), Hecate appeared with an electric star on her forehead and an off-stage chorus sang words from Middleton's *Witch* to a 'fine wild melody'. The sky was lit by lightning flashes and blood-coloured exhalations and, in conclusion, some sixty witches appeared to fly through the air. For the siege of Dunsinane in the last of six Acts the scene moved repeatedly from outside to inside the castle, with crowds of soldiers crossing and re-crossing the stage to keep the pace moving as fast as possible. Hughes notes, from the *Pall Mall Budget*, that '165 costumes were made for soldiers (designed in batches of 10), 115 Scottish and 50 English.' Here, as elsewhere, Irving managed crowds of supernumeraries and cumbersome sets through trusted assistants and his own personal vigilance. While seeking to captivate the audience with impressive sights and sounds, his over-riding concerns were to light the two principal actors and ensure that the pace of every element encouraged the closest attention for the finer moments of their performances. In production and performance, the Lyceum *Macbeth* anticipated many of the same kind of achievements that are sought by present-day directors and designers, although its use of them would seem overly sentimental and melodramatic today.

## Laurence Olivier

In several ways Olivier's 1955 Macbeth was the heir of Irving's. He was an experienced Shakespearean actor who had tackled Macbeth some years earlier; he had also managed his own theatre company and starred in it with his wife, Vivien Leigh. Now he was acting with an unfamiliar company but, like Irving's, one more permanent than his own had been, and he was working with a director, Glen Byam Shaw, but he held his own view of Macbeth's character, one that had similarities to Irving's. For Olivier also, it was a 'domestic tragedy' in which the partners go very different ways, but his Macbeth knows what is going to happen, from the moment he sees the first Witch, and she foresees nothing.

> The man has imagination and the woman has none. . . . That's what gives her the enormous courage to plot the whole thing, force him into it, persuade him, cajole him, bully him, tease him into it. . . . It's the passage of two people, one going up and one going down. And there comes a moment when he 'looks at her and he realizes that she can't take it any more, and he goes on and she goes down.    (Interview in *Great Acting*, ed. Hal Burton, 1967)

In keeping with this view of the tragedy, Vivien Leigh's Lady Macbeth could have little in common with Ellen Terry's, and Olivier portrayed a man whose thought and feeling were as one: the torment of failure and guilt was felt throughout his entire being, not poeticized as Irving had played the role.

The stage set by Roger Furse was spacious, dark, and gothic, with many jagged details and several levels; thrones and crowns were large and lumpish; it changed frequently from castle to castle, interior to exterior. The costumes were vaguely and glamorously medieval. The director took pains to bring the whole company in line, with movements he had worked out ahead of time. The cast was strong, the older members experienced: for example, William Devlin, as Ross, had previously played leading roles. The youngest actors would in future take major roles at Stratford and elsewhere: Ian Holm, as Donalbain, would be Richard the Third, Prince Hal, Henry the Fifth, and, many years later, King Lear at the National. But neither staging nor supporting cast made an impression as memorable as Olivier's physical presence, his voice, his silences, his eyes: his tireless re-working of action and words. In his forty-eighth year, he was at the height of his powers.

A chorus of approval identified what *The Times* called 'a soul in torment'. This was not expressed in sustained poetic utterance but in many small, intimate details. The same critic noted that, in comforting his wife, 'a note of resentment against crime's awful necessities creeps into his ironic, "Then be thou jocund." ' Harold Hobson in the *Sunday Times* saw that:

> This Macbeth briefs the murderers of Banquo with a contempt for their trade which is exceeded by his contempt for himself, a contempt the more arresting because it is tinged with a bitter amusement.

Almost all reviewers wrote about short passages of text and the physicality of Olivier's performance. Kenneth Tynan of the *Observer* relished the sensuous and moral ending of the tragedy:

> Sir Laurence's throttled fury switches into top gear, and we see him, baffled but still colossal. 'I 'gin to be a-weary of the sun' held the very ecstasy of despair, the actor swaying with grief, his voice rising like hair on the crest of a trapped animal.

In the *Daily Mail*, Cecil Wilson explained:

> Sir Laurence, squeezing out every word, syllable by syllable, lurches through his murders in a conscience-stricken nightmare, his face white with the loss of other men's blood, his eyes staring with lack of sleep and his voice mounting to a desperate tenor as guilt envelops him.

The performance had an inner stillness, a self-awareness that seemed to hold back in self-judgement. Before he said ' 'Twas a rough night' in answer to young Lennox's account of 'strange screams of death' in the 'unruly night' (II.iii.51–8), he seemed to steady his whole being by an act of will until he had found a response he could speak with an assumed ease that was close to amusement.

Olivier took time to establish the sensations that lie behind speech, not a sub-text co-existent with the spoken word but a pre-text that alone could force utterance and make the words seem necessary, a conscious effort without which he could not proceed. When he wished that the killing of Duncan might be a 'blow' that was 'the be-all and the end-all here' (I.vii.4–5), his words seemed to have taken him too far and too fast: he stopped and in a forced and calculated repetition added, 'But here'. Then he stopped again as if he saw himself standing still and palpable, caught until a pun and a physical image gave him release:

> . . . the end-all here [*pause*]
> But *here* [*pause*] upon this bank and shoal of time,
> We'd jump the life to come.

Olivier came down-stage right, as close as he could to his audience, and was held still until he could energize *jump* and turn *life to come* into a denigrating dismissal. The third *here*, which soon follows, caused no hesitation, as if he had already entered through a narrow passage into a new and terrifying world where thoughts and imagination both compelled and enchained him:

> But in these cases
> We still have judgement here – that we but teach
> Bloody instructions, . . .

The production offered its audience a progressive experience. The horror, violence, sacrilege, superstition, and machinations of the narrative – even its evil or immorality – were all underplayed. The entire production served to open up the very being of a murderer who wished for all the good things of life, respected 'gracious' qualities in others, and was left with no other option but to 'try the last' when he finds himself isolated and facing retribution. Its originality lay in Olivier's conviction that the right to say each one of Shakespeare's words had to be earned with both body and mind. Because of that effort, he held his audience's rapt attention. Earlier actors, Irving and Garrick chief among them, had made the text their own but seldom if ever had they grasped and used the treacherous nature of words as Olivier did – in a way that Beckett, Pinter and others did when beginning to write plays in the mid-1950s.

Centred on the inner consciousness of a man responsible for his own suffering, it was a performance of its time, as good theatre will always be. Every other element of the play gave way to that. The witches were elaborately presented but had little relationship with the man they cursed:

> for all their shrill emphasis they are reduced to nasty hags scampering round an unpleasant dish . . . the producer makes a great point of our seeing the fillet of a fenny snake, the root of hemlock digged i' the dark, and other ingredients of their recipe.     (*Coventry Evening Telegraph*)

Neither the tragedy's violence nor its cruelty was given prominence. For example, the political imperatives of the army mustering against Macbeth were cut from the acting text: the bringing of 'medicine' to heal the 'sickly weal' and the sacrifice of blood 'To dew the sovereign flower, and drown the weeds' (V.ii.27–30). Also cut was Macduff's insistence that 'just censures' should be brought to the 'true event', along with 'industrious soldiership' (V.iv.14–16). Still more amazingly, as if the well-being of a nation was of no consequence to an audience still emerging from the Second World War, all of Macduff's words were cut as he seeks the 'tyrant' who has killed his wife and children and turned soldiers into 'wretched kerns' (V.vi.24–33). Visually, the production bore no resemblance to any political or everyday reality in the manner of later productions; it all took place in a fantasy world, sombre but improbable.

## Trevor Nunn, Ian McKellen and Judi Dench

The Royal Shakespeare Company's *Macbeth* at The Other Place at Stratford-upon-Avon in 1976 was startlingly unlike any earlier production. The very origin of this *Macbeth* was unexpected because it was the result of failure. Two years earlier Trevor Nunn had directed the same play, with Nicol Williamson as Macbeth, in the main theatre at Stratford and managed to please no one while trying hard to do so – the witches, for example, swung from chandeliers. He staged the production again at the Aldwych Theatre in London, stripped of its visual excesses, and that had worked no better. Now he took the way pioneered a few years earlier by Buzz Goodbody in her production of *Hamlet*.

This director, recently recruited to the company straight from the University of Sussex, had used the simplest and cheapest of means and the smallest practicable cast to stage her production – in fact, this was all she was able to use. The famous tragedy was presented on a shallow platform against plain white screens in what had been a make-shift performance space, and played each time to no more than a few hundred spectators. The director had used resources like those of a student or fringe show except that they were backed by a large organization and cast with experienced and talented actors. Quite as important as that, Buzz Goodbody was a person with keen intelligence who assumed that theatre should speak to the present time and the world in which she lived.

The Other Space *Hamlet* was widely acclaimed so that, by following in her footsteps, the Artistic Director of the RSC was playing from a position of strength, and by relying on some of theatre's most basic resources, he was to rediscover and give new life to *Macbeth*. The small audience encircled the stage on two levels, each only two or three rows deep, so that all the action happened only feet away. At this close range, every spectator experienced the play's physical embodiment with a compelling immediacy. A filmed version of the production is now widely available but that cannot reproduce the sense of involvement and discovery that was shared between everyone in the theatre.

Something of the quality of the production's first performance can be gained from quoting the unusually vivid and detailed reviews. In contrast to their responses to earlier productions of this play, the critics had comparatively little new to say about the interpretation of crucial lines of the text or about the motivation of the two principals. They were mostly concerned with recording how Trevor Nunn had used the intimate setting to introduce stage business that created a believable context for the action, and to obtain central performances that were powerfully driven and finely detailed, rather than grand or oratorical. The production opposed the sacred against the profane . . . with organ music and a sanctimonious hush emphasizing the legitimacy of Duncan's rule and with foul chanting, shrieks and demonic possession greeting Macbeth as he arrives among the weird sisters.    (Ned Chaillet, *The Times*)

The haunted feast [was] an ambitious combination of [the] laughing bravado, foaming rage, and grotesque mimicry of the genial host: a pseudo-playful slap of someone's cheek, a woozy wave at the departing guests.    (Benedict Nightingale, *New Statesman*)

Macbeth at Dunsinane stands beneath a single light bulb; on 'I 'gin to be aweary of the sun' [V.v.49], he shoves it, sets it swinging backwards and forwards, so that it illuminates his face only on alternate beats; seizing it again, he shines it on to a talisman kept in his hand since his last meeting with the witches. . . .    (Robert Cushman, *Observer*)

Little in the production was conventionally spectacular. The stage was bare except for a circle marked on the floor and some empty crates. For the feast, actors carried their own crates onto the stage to sit on; the ghost of Banquo made no entry but was seen only by Macbeth as it sat on one of the crates. The witches raised no apparitions but seized their drugged victim and stripped off his clothes to mark his body with magic symbols before showing ragged dolls as they spoke the prophecies; then Macbeth was blindfolded and the show of kings existed only in his mind. No armies marched in the final Act but their presence and orders were heard from off-stage as Macbeth surrounded himself with piles of crates. His severed head could not be displayed at such close quarters and so Macduff entered with two bloody daggers in his hands.

By focusing the audience's attention down onto small details the wider context of the narrative was mostly forgotten, and consequently its improbabilities and arcane superstitions were accepted as if they were real. Costumes were modern, the weapons daggers, rather than swords; jack boots and black leather represented military dress, and not cumbersome armour. Throughout the production sensation and physical activity counted far more than the appearance or real-life behaviour. By these means, the remote and historical was made believable, actual, and very obviously present.

Performance was also intensely dramatic and the director had paced its development with great care.

The progressive separation of man and wife, as they reacted differently to the collapse of their attempt to seize power, was shown very clearly and their ultimate defeat thoroughly depicted. At the start, Judi Dench as Lady Macbeth exerted a powerful sexual influence over her husband and used it to hold him to their earlier decision and propel him towards murder, but, finding 'her support brusquely rejected once he has come to power, she is a shattered ghost by the time she has to officiate at the otherwise ghostless feast' (Jack Tinker, *Daily Mail*). At the start, 'in thick darkness', Ian McKellen as Macbeth:

> prowls with tigerish vitality. After the murder, the daggers rattle in his hands. After the coronation, he exchanges a hideous corkscrew smile with his wife. . . . By the end, the evil within has made him a hollow man: empty, weary, flaccid, all hope gone.    (John Barber, *Daily Telegraph*)

Little evidence can be found that this Macbeth lived the haunted life of Laurence Olivier's extraordinarily gifted warrior, or that he endured the torture of Irving's sensitive but cold-hearted and ruthless warrior. McKellen acted the isolation and defeat of an intensely driven leader who is hungry for power and possesses a keen and dangerous mind. By her very presence Judi Dench's Lady Macbeth could project her will, but once she finds herself alone, she becomes helpless. The context for action was neither the Gothic show-case of Byam Shaw's production with the Oliviers nor the huge representations of wild terrains and remote castles of Irving's, with its cast of hundreds. It was a stripped and closely observed space, full of dramatic and intensely realized action and little else of any substance. The production amazed and enthralled with its highly dramatic nightmare images in black, off-set with a few less effectual images of holiness in white. The intensity of the central performances and the interplay between the fourteen actors, drawn from a company working together for long seasons, eclipsed the power and conviction of any other staging of the play that its audiences could have remembered.

## Gregory Doran, Antony Sher and Harriet Walter

When Gregory Doran's 1999 Stratford production arrived the next year at the Young Vic Theatre in London its success was assured and all the tickets had sold in advance. Its star performer took artistic risks in his stride and its company of eighteen alternately stormed and processed across a blackened stage that reached out among the audience. Lighting would sometimes change startlingly but was often dim, with shafts of light breaking through; the play started in darkness. Drumming repeatedly drove the action forward or supplemented dramatic tension. When the production had opened at the Swan Theatre, the smaller of the two main houses at Stratford, it was hailed by a critical chorus of approval as 'thrilling', 'gripping', a 'tremendous production [that] explodes with an elemental force', and 'the most exciting, most compelling' since Trevor Nunn's of more than twenty years earlier; it had 'moved with the murderously incisive swiftness of a slasher knife'. Now, in May 2000, it was said that, 'Even if the rollercoaster pace gives little pause for thought or emotional response, the sensory exhilaration echoes that of the protagonists themselves' (Patrick Marmion, *Time Out*).

From Nunn's production, Doran had taken an intimate performance space and a small compact company, but quickening the pace and adding more sound effects. In place of an intensely realized credibility, he provided excitement and shock. Together with his leading actor he had made many bold decisions. Costumes were reminiscent of modern warfare in dangerous political conditions, with soldiers in grey combat gear, berets and revolvers, and showing signs of battle. While everyone, except Duncan, the women, and young children, appeared in modern military uniforms, no consistent or recognizable political situation was established on stage. The programme carried an essay by Fergal Keane, the Irish journalist, that drew parallels to the play's violence from Kosovo, the Congo, East Timor, and Iraq, but the production avoided all precise references. Instead the production presented a character study of a hyperactive and mentally unstable soldier of the present time who was experienced and successful in battle, gleeful in action, and sardonic in thought: a person who could horrify others while failing to be sensitive to horror himself. In other words, the play became a study of military corruption with no specific political message. *The Tragedy of Macbeth*, giving 'little pause for thought or emotional response', seemed on the point of becoming a pacifist cartoon with some similarities to horror comics and violent video games.

Paradoxically, this downgrading in style and content was accomplished with notable skill, resource, and invention: the thoughtfulness of the enterprise was not in question. The play-text had been revalued, as it has been many times before, and had revealed unforeseen qualities in performance. These could be identified by newly invented stage business and line-readings that flouted tradition. Banquo and Macbeth first come on stage:

> hoisted like heroes on the shoulders of their chanting comrades and Sher, laughingly mad-eyed and with his blood up, lets you see that, for Macbeth, this civil war in Scotland has been a liberating experience. (Paul Taylor, *The Independent*)

Macbeth laughs when he first sees the Witches and, after he has murdered Duncan, his remark ''Twas a rough night' is spoken with dark humour.

> He can end the still more awesome passage about wading ever-deeper in blood with an ironic chuckle. You don't feel his mind is full of scorpions, as he claims, or even dizzy with insomnia, as his wife suggests. (Benedict Nightingale, *The Times*)

Reviewers often caught a volatile mixture of eagerness and deflation in the way he spoke. For example, with 'To be thus is nothing,' when he has attained the crown, 'a whole world of feeling is compressed into that "nothing" – impatience, disappointment, self-mockery, the businesslike contemplation of future evil' (John Gross, *Sunday Telegraph*). 'Tomorrow, and tomorrow' is 'the throw-away remark of one who has finally seen his bluff called' (Carole Woddis, *The Herald*). The tragedy was not about guilt or ambition, and still less about a marriage. Nor was it much about 'supernatural soliciting', the witches appearing as vagrants left on the field of battle; they were involved in some unlikely trickery but their speech and rituals were unimpressive. The director and Antony Sher, his Macbeth, were concerned with other matters: on one level, performance and production displayed the deranged behaviour of a successful soldier, and, on a more thoughtful one, the death of conscience.

Within an otherwise single-minded production, two elements stood out against the strong current of its innovation. No one could miss the different contact with the audience when Stephen Noonan as the Porter came forward and started to improvise with and around the words of the text. While he was alone on stage, an easy complicity sprang up between actor and audience that was in steep contrast to the forceful, inescapable effect of the production's technically accomplished stage-management, its well rehearsed pacing, and the co-ordinated responses of its actors. The Porter was a reminder of a technically simpler, more open kind of theatre that, by its very nature, is more precise and more topical in representing events of the day. Among the ad libbing and talk with the audience, 'equivocation' of the text became political spin, and time was made for an imitation of Tony Blair trying to use the latest buzzword that has been fed to him by Alistair Campbell.

The other major counter-statement was Harriet Walter's Lady Macbeth, so far left out of this account. Not that the actor was being rebellious. As Sher was an increasingly mad-brained military commander, she was a confined and constrained soldier's wife who as the action ran out of hand was unable to support him or maintain her own self-control; by the end she could scarcely speak her own thoughts. This reading of the text was well suited to the director's purposes and received a finely detailed performance:

> She has a superb cold authority: her analysis of her husband's scruples is detached rather than scornful. But the self-command isn't overdone: you always sense the ordinary mortal behind it, the woman who eventually cracks. (*Sunday Telegraph*)

Lady Macbeth invited a far closer attention to the play than was called for elsewhere and needed more time to be sure of sufficient response. Critics were less sure of their ground here and far from unanimous. The role Harriet Walter had been given to play came from a highly refined theatre that stages Beckett and Pinter: silence and stillness were needed if her performance was to be appreciated. It looked backward for its models and was at odds with the production's basically violent, melodramatic and harshly comic style of playing. Little contact was possible between man and wife.

## Recent adaptations

During the last fifty or more years, many influences have been at work in theatres around the world and most of them can be seen in productions of *Macbeth*. The more visual and sensual medium of cinema has encouraged theatre productions to emphasize the sexual relationship of the two principals. On her first appearance Lady Macbeth has been shown lying on a bed while she reads or re-reads her husband's letter, and he goes to her there when he returns with new honours from war. A large bed may remain on stage throughout the play to be featured whenever the two are together in private, and later, for the sleepwalking scene and, again, for her death.

Another kind of production has given prominence to the Witches by elaborating their rituals with or without the songs from Middleton's *The Witch*. Sometimes they return in Act V to watch their prophecies being fulfilled and then to celebrate Macbeth's death with more rituals and dance. Hecat has sung her long speech in Act III, scene v, after descending from high above the stage, as goddesses did in Renaissance masques and early operas; the Witches will be silent and awestruck until they join together in song as their mistress makes her exit. Other productions have emphasized every textual reference to Christian thought and observances: religious music and formal postures for prayer, submission, or the giving and receiving of blessing are introduced wherever possible. The Witches play a conspicuously blasphemous role, with perverted rituals and desecrated crosses or effigies. At the close, Malcolm is on his knees when he dedicates himself to kingship and calls upon the 'grace of Grace' to support his autocratic decisions. Devotional singing concludes the tragedy, not the sound of trumpets or a salute with weapons and military banners.

Whenever the text has been translated into non-European languages similar changes of emphasis have occurred as the text reflects other cultures. Kingship, heroism, marital relations, attitudes to death and inheritance, national and personal loyalties, religion and superstition, belief and doubt, are among the major issues in the play that will register differently when not performed in English. While the majority of translated texts have only local and topical validity, a few have had more permanent lives in touring productions. A 1980 *Macbeth* by Yukio Ninagawa in Tokyo was frequently revived for a series of world tours; as late as 1998 it was re-produced to open a new theatre in Tokyo. Although staged in Japanese, with many elements taken from ancient Japanese society and many symbols and devices from its theatre practice, the director's sensational modern stagecraft and repeated use of Gabriel Fauré's *Requiem Mass* made this much-altered version readily accessible wherever it was presented. A lasting record was made on videotape in 1985 and is still available.

An even greater longevity has been enjoyed by *Umabatha*, written in English by Welcome Msomi and published in Pretoria in 1997. Beginning life at the University of Natal in 1970, the author's own production was further developed for the 1972 World Theatre Season at the Aldwych Theatre in London and for subsequent tours in North America. Another revival was for the opening season of the new Globe Theatre on Bankside, London, in 1997. Its success was largely due to the irresistible appeal of the strong rhythms of Zulu drumming, chanting and dancing that accompanied and sustained much of the action. Carried along by this impetus, witchcraft was presented without apology, as if it were a part of everyday life, and with an energy that spilt over into laughter. For audiences outside Africa all this and the costumes had an exotic interest, but the drilling and choreography of the dances, a designer's hand and eye in the costuming, and a director's control of performances were indebted to large-scale commercial musicals, both North American and South African.

*Macbeth* has also been altered for theatrical convenience, some roles being cut and others doubled or trebled so that it can be acted by no more than five actors and with minimal staging and scenic support. Tom Stoppard's duplex drama *Dogg's Hamlet, Cahoot's*

*Macbeth* (1979) includes part of such a text that is a good indication of what skilful and witty cutting can achieve. This greatly reduced *Macbeth* was devised in response to being told of a five-person performance of the play in living rooms in Czechoslovakia during the Soviet occupation when the theatres were closed. Most abbreviated versions are produced to reduce costs and casts so that the play can be taken on tour to schools and colleges or the smallest theatrical venues, none of which could accommodate a full-scale production, or afford to pay for it. The wish of actors to perform this text is also a major reason for the popularity of these mini-versions.

With surprising frequency Shakespeare's text has also been cut, rearranged, and rewritten so that it becomes an almost entirely different play. Lady Macbeth has been made the central figure of a dance-drama, the other parts, including that of her husband, being relegated to minor or entirely silent roles. Macbeth, Lady Macbeth, the Macduff family, Malcolm, and the Witches have all become figures of myth that can be borrowed to illuminate the issues of the present time. The original is likely to be left far behind and a new play created that follows the broad outline of Shakespeare's plot and with enough of the original dialogue to emphasize and illuminate parallels between the new subject matter and the old. Most of these adaptations are not durable and, having filled theatres in their own time and place, now live only in printed form: for example, *Macbird!* which won awards in 1967 for its satire of President Lyndon Johnson. Another example is Charles Marowitz's *A Macbeth* of 1969, which had three Macbeths, a Lady Macbeth who announces her own death, the customary three Witches, and only four other named parts. This version exploited the actors' inventiveness and physical skills, its success being due to the author-director's handling of them and his invention of a new dramatic structure while using only the words found in Shakespeare's play. Eugène Ionesco's *Macbett*, produced in Paris in 1972, is a broadly comic, violent, and political parody, a rewriting that is still available in print but unlikely to be seen again in performance.

During the last half of the twentieth century and beyond, new versions and adaptations of *Macbeth* have succeeded each other in an unstoppable tide. As this book is being read, there is every chance that this old play is being re-formed and rewritten for tomorrow's audiences, so strong is its action and so challenging the image of our lives that it brings onto a stage, dominated by two contrasted characters who are deeply involved with each other.

# 5  The Play on Screen

The nature of the medium means that no film version of Shakespeare's plays can offer its viewer an experience equivalent to a stage performance but one in its own right and working in its own way. With *Macbeth*, this is especially true because of the play's intensity of focus and the strange, uncanny nature of the Witches. A reader with little or no opportunity of seeing *Macbeth* in a theatre should seek out two or three of the readily available screen versions whose different qualities will complement one another.

The 1957 Japanese film *The Throne of Blood* is a masterpiece, still available for purchase and found in many Shakespeare libraries. Directed by Akira Kurosawa in black and white and performed in Japanese with English subtitles, its major changes to the play's story and principal characters are immediately obvious. Having chosen to set the action in the military and autocratic society of sixteenth-century Japan, Kurosawa was able to create powerful images that can help a reader of the play to envisage it in action. The film's barren landscape, with long distances that must be travelled alone on horseback, corresponds to the play's Scotland and its 'blasted heath' (I.iii.77) more closely than the natural world we live in today or are likely to know from personal experience. Toshiro Mifune, who plays Washizu, the character corresponding to Macbeth, portrays a strongly built warrior-lord who has absolute authority over many people and commands a large army. He is ruthless in exercise of this power and orders his men to fight without doubting his right to do so. Ancient Japanese armour and formal customs make him an unfamiliar figure for us today but when he is obeyed without hesitation or prepares himself for battle he has much in common with elements of Shakespeare's Macbeth that we find hard to imagine. The scale and inaccessibility of this warlord's castle provide images for the approach of Malcolm's army to Macbeth's castle at Dunsinane, which, according to Cathness, he 'strongly fortifies' (V.ii.12). In Holinshed Shakespeare had read a detailed description of the forced labour used in this work (see p. 108) and this film shows us what this might have entailed.

The alterations made to Shakespeare's handling of the story pinpoint difficulties that Shakespeare must also have met. Replacing his Witches, the film shows a single old woman unexpectedly encountered, who is mysterious but makes only small visual impact and so removes the display manifestations of this alternative source of knowledge and power in the world. Instead of walking and talking in her sleep, Lady Macbeth sits silently in isolation, washing her hands; when Macbeth visits her in these last moments, she does not, or cannot, recognize him. With no Macduff to seek revenge, the end of the tragedy is very different, a popular uprising and military *coup d'état*, rather than a personal crisis of self-belief. The hero, deserted by his army, is killed by many arrows shot by unseen soldiers.

Roman Polanski's *Macbeth* of 1971 stays much closer to Shakespeare's text but viewers are likely to find that Macbeth's kingdom is portrayed in more familiar terms than are appropriate for the Scotland of the play. This is a period costume epic set in a colourful and extensive landscape, with a photogenic hero and heroine (Jon Finch and Francesca Annis) supported by numerous supers in its closing episodes. The bloody captain early in the film, Banquo's murder and bloody ghost at Macbeth's feast, and, later, the extended violence used to terrify and kill Lady Macduff with her children and servants, are likely to have made a stronger impression when the film was made than they do today now that they are in competition with many films of more brutal and life-like cruelty. The images of real-life casualties and terror that we see daily on television in our own homes are enough to render this once horrific film unreal and tame in our eyes. When Macduff strikes off Macduff's head at the end of the play, what once may have carried conviction is likely to register today as an expertly contrived trick.

For a reader of Shakespeare's play unable to see it performed on stage, the chief merits of this film are that it tells the story visually in ways that can be easily followed and that its shortened and rearranged text is spoken so that every word is clearly heard. Unfortunately this is at the cost of strong feelings, depth of commitment, and moments of insecurity. A sequence of fighting hand to hand with several assailants precedes Macbeth's death so that it becomes an occasion for (improbable) swordplay rather than self-awareness or reappraisal. A similar devaluation of inner experience runs throughout the film: for instance, when Macbeth speaks his first words, 'So fair and foul a day I have not seen,' rain is pouring down so that the words seem like a remark about the weather.

This film, like Kurosawa's, has trouble depicting witchcraft but does not find such a radical solution. Three crones utter their words and handle some of the objects they name without building expectation or establishing any ritual gravity. A lot of smoke, cackling, and dim lighting accompany the apparitions of the play's Act IV, scene i, and so render them stagey rather than impressive. Lady Macbeth's sleepwalking had again given trouble, which Polanski solved by having her appear naked, totally visible for one brief moment, and by adding an entirely new scene to keep her in the film for longer than in Shakespeare's play. Unlike a Japanese film maker, Polanski could not write more text for her to speak, so she is shown weeping as she again reads the letter Macbeth had sent at the beginning. That both these films find a way to extend Lady Macbeth's role prompts the question why Shakespeare should have ended it before Macbeth returns to the stage for the challenging and decisive end of his role.

The film that most strongly contrasts with these two and best complements them is Trevor Nunn's video version of his stage production that was described in the previous section. It suffers from being inexpensively made and shot against a totally black background that gives no sense of place and little of space or the time of day or night. Instead of filming take by take, only a few months were spent on the film. But it has the great advantage of an entire cast experienced in performing Shakespeare's plays and led by two actors pre-eminent in their profession. The company had presented this production many times in various theatres during the previous three years. The actors had had time to become at ease with the text and had explored its many possibilities in performance. Each of them had developed his or her own understanding and grasp of the person they played. They could take risks and rapidly change from being thoughtful to giving way to emotion, from being open to suggestion to being isolated and closed in mind – necessary talents for responding to the rapidly changing dialogue of this tragedy.

The same circumstances were also responsible for the film's considerable shortcomings. The production had lost both the stage and the closely encircling audience of its early performances (see above, pp. 128–30); as captured on camera, the performances are occasionally overwrought. Besides, having no context in which to film the action, there being no set or exterior scenes, the camera for much of the time shows little more than faces lit against the unvarying black background. Often only one face fills the screeen, and sometimes only its mouth or eyes. These features are almost continually expressive, as such details seldom are in Polanski's and Kurosawa's films, but the advantage is lessened because the whole presence of an actor is seldom seen. When two characters are talking or fighting with each other only a small portion of their bodies is likely to be visible. Shakespeare's texts played on a stage summon the whole beings of the actors to participate in the ongoing drama and that engagement Trevor Nunn's screen version cannot show – even though it had been called upon in rehearsal and theatrical performances. At best, the total commitment of the performances is implicit in how the words are spoken and in the film's frequent silences, but even then it is not easily appreciated and sometimes seems false or unconvincing.

What this film does commandingly show is the inner anguish of Macbeth: what Shakespeare has him call the fears that 'stick deep . . . rancours / In the vessel of my peace' or, later, 'torture of the mind . . . [and] restless ecstacy'. Ian McKellen accepts these challenges and brings astonishing intensity and force to his performance, as if he were on the brink of losing control. Judi Dench's Lady Macbeth has the cooler mind that knows that these 'deeds must not be thought / After these ways; so, it will make us mad.' Her performance is more still and quiet than McKellen's; the breakdown is within, as tears rise to the eyes and suffering is heard in the voice. Her sleepwalking is not altered beyond what the text can support, as it is in the other two films considered here, but her single 'O!', at which the Doctor says, 'What a sigh was there,' is long drawn out, with its intensity increasing rather than losing power. Her 'What's done cannot be undone' expresses a tortured mind rather than fatalism.

The film's black background and its isolation of a few figures – the acting company is no more numerous than it was in the theatre – are at their greatest disadvantage in Shakespeare's crowd scenes. The 'most admired disorder' of the guests at the banquet is represented by a few torsos and heads, hardly moving and making little sound. The capture of Dunsinane at the end has little visible effect beyond a flagging pace; there is no sign that Macbeth is surrounded by an army so that there is no place to which he can fly. No bloody head is displayed; instead Ross holds the crown and Macduff enters with bloody hands. The Witches are presented in much the same way as in the theatre production but, without an encircling and attentive audience and with no sense of using a restricted space, the effect of what they do is greatly diminished and tends to seem trivial. What makes the strongest impression and stays in the mind is the contrasting psychic energy of the tragedy's hero and heroine and the haunting quality of the words they speak.

After seeing any of these films, one of the readily available audio recordings of the whole text will remind the viewer of what has been left out or rearranged and, the visual imagination having been prompted by seeing a least some of the action, the listener will have a better idea of what the text requires actors to do, and should be able to supply a fuller sense of the play's physical embodiment.

# 6 Critical Assessments

No one can adequately describe *The Tragedy of Macbeth*, and to assess its achievements is still more difficult. Nevertheless, as the commentary in this book has shown, this text repeatedly requires actors and readers to make their own judgements about the meaning of words as they respond to them and before they speak them. The play is so written that it *asks* to be held in the mind and awaken the imagination of everyone who reads it. A professional critic of the twenty-first century, who uses a range of new critical terms and pursues specific issues that were unknown to Shakespeare and his contemporaries, is not trespassing on the play but developing reactions that the text invites and positively encourages.

When starting to respond critically to the text a good plan is to identify the most obvious lines of enquiry and use the simplest of means. Shakespeare's earliest critics are useful here because their terms are readily understood and, having listened to them, we can then turn to what has been said on the same questions by critics closer to our own times, who are likely to bring much the same interests as ourselves. In the last hundred or more years, so many and so various judgements have been made that this book has no space for a full hearing of any one of them. A selected number are therefore represented and in the next section, on 'Further Reading', bibliographical details are given for following up each citation.

The short notice for *Macbeth* in *The Companion to the Playhouse* (1764), by David Erskine Baker and others, gives an early assessment that can serve to open up the basic lines of approach:

This play is extremely irregular, every one of the rules of the drama being entirely and repeatedly broken in upon. Yet, notwithstanding, it contains an infinity of beauties, both with respect to language, character, passion and incident. The incantations of the Witches are equal, if not superior, to the *Canidia* of Horace. The use this author has made of Banquo's Ghost towards the heightening the already heated imagination of Macbeth, is inimitably fine. Lady Macbeth discovering her own crimes in her sleep, is perfectly original and admirably conducted.

Macbeth's soliloquies both before and after the murder, are master-pieces of unmatchable writing; while his readiness of being deluded at first by the Witches, and his desperation on the discovery of the fatal ambiguity and loss of all hope from supernatural predictions, produce a catastrophe truly just, and form'd with the utmost judgment. In a word, not withstanding all its irregularities, it is certain one of the best pieces of the very best master in this kind of writing that the World ever produced.

While this writer struggles to find superlatives, he identifies the play's characteristics in its use of words, its characters, themes, structure and plot, and its theatrical sensations and irregularities. These were to be the recurrent concerns of criticism, and the incidents that this critic dwells on continued to be primary centres of interest.

## Verbal language

As soon as editors started to annotate the texts, discussing variant readings and explaining 'hard' words, unusual references, obsolete idioms and syntax, Shakespeare's use of language in the play became widely discussed in other ways than praise for its beauties. A. C. Bradley, who became famed for his analysis of Shakespeare's tragic heroes, was at least as original in his examination of this play's imagery and the 'tone' or 'atmosphere' that derives from the language. And he studied words in relation to visual language, narrative, and structure: the thoroughness of his engagement with the words of the text was unprecedented. Extensive quotation is needed to show the great step forward that his criticism made in this respect:

> In many parts of *Macbeth* there is in the language a peculiar compression, pregnancy, energy, even violence; the harmonious grace and even flow, often conspicuous in *Hamlet*, have almost disappeared. The chief characters,

built on a scale at least as large as that of *Othello*, seem to attain at times an almost superhuman stature. The diction has in places a huge and rugged grandeur, which degenerates here and there into timidity. The solemn majesty of the royal Ghost in *Hamlet*, appearing in armour and standing silent in the moonlight, is exchanged for shapes of horror, dimly seen in the murky air or revealed by the glare of the caldron fire in a dark cavern, or for the ghastly face of Banquo badged with blood and staring with blank eyes. The other three tragedies all open with conversations which lead into the action: here the action bursts into wild life amidst the sounds of a thunderstorm and the echoes of a distant battle. It hurries through seven very brief scenes of mounting suspense to a terrible crisis, which is reached, in the murder of Duncan, at the beginning of the Second Act. Pausing a moment and changing its shape, it hastes again with scarcely diminished speed to fresh horrors. And even when the speed of the outward action is slackened, the same effect is continued in another form: we are shown a soul tortured by an agony which admits not a moment's repose, and rushing in frenzy towards its doom. *Macbeth* is very much shorter than the other three tragedies, but our experience in traversing it is so crowded and intense that it leaves an impression not of brevity but of speed. It is the most vehement, the most concentrated, perhaps we may say the most tremendous, of the tragedies.

A Shakespearean tragedy, as a rule, has a special tone or atmosphere of its own, quite perceptible, however difficult to describe. The effect of this atmosphere is marked with unusual strength in *Macbeth*. It is due to a variety of influences which combine with those just noticed, so that, acting and reacting, they form a whole; and the desolation of the blasted heath, the design of the Witches, the guilt in the hero's soul, the darkness of the night, seem to emanate from one and the same source. This effect is strengthened by a multitude of small touches, which at the moment may be little noticed but still leave their mark on the imagination. We may approach the consideration of the characters and the action by distinguishing some of the ingredients of this general effect.

Darkness, we may even say blackness, broods over this tragedy. It is remarkable that almost all the scenes which at once recur to memory take place either at night or in some dark spot. The vision of the dagger, the murder of Duncan, the murder of Banquo, the sleepwalking of Lady Macbeth, all come in nightscenes. The Witches dance in the thick air of a storm, or, 'black and midnight hags', receive Macbeth in a cavern. The blackness of night is to the hero a thing of fear, even of horror; and that which he feels becomes the spirit of the play. The faint glimmerings of the western sky at twilight are here menacing: it is the hour when the traveller hastens to reach safety in his inn and when Banquo rides homeward to meet his assassins; the hour when 'light thickens', when 'night's black agents to their prey do rouse', when the wolf begins to howl, and the owl to scream, and withered murder steals forth to his work. Macbeth bids the stars hide their fires that his 'black' desires may be concealed; Lady Macbeth calls on thick night to come, palled in the dunnest smoke of hell. The moon is down and no stars shine when Banquo, dreading the dreams of the coming night, goes unwillingly to bed, and leaves Macbeth to wait for the summons of the little bell. When the next day should dawn, its light is 'strangled', and 'darkness does the face of earth entomb'. In the whole drama the sun seems to shine only twice; first, in the beautiful but ironical passage where Duncan sees the swallows flitting round the castle of death; and, afterwards, when at the close the avenging army gathers to rid the earth of its shame. Of the many slighter touches which deepen this effect I notice only one. The failure of nature in Lady Macbeth is marked by her fear of darkness; 'she has light by her continually'. And in the one phrase of fear that escapes her lips even in sleep, it is of the darkness of the place of torment that she speaks.

The atmosphere of *Macbeth*, however, is not that of unrelieved blackness. On the contrary, as compared with *King Lear* and its cold dim gloom, *Macbeth* leaves a decided impression of colour; it is really the impression of a black night broken by flashes of light and colour, sometimes vivid and even glaring. They are the lights and colours of the thunderstorm in the first scene; of the dagger hanging before Macbeth's eyes and glittering alone in the midnight air; of the torch borne by the servant when he and his lord come upon Banquo crossing the castlecourt to his room; of the torch, again, which Fleance carried to light his father to death, and which was dashed out by one of the murderers; of the torches that flared in the hall on the face of the Ghost and the blanched cheeks of Macbeth; of the flames beneath the boiling caldron from which the apparitions in the cavern rose; of the taper which showed to the Doctor and Gentlewoman the wasted face and blank eyes of Lady Macbeth. And, above all, the colour is the colour of blood. It cannot be an accident that the image of blood is forced upon us continually, not merely by the events themselves, but by full descriptions, and even by reiteration of the word in unlikely parts of the dialogue. The Witches, after their first wild appearance, have hardly quitted the stage when there staggers onto it a 'bloody man', gashed with wounds. His tale is of a hero whose 'brandished steel smoked with bloody execution', 'carved out a passage' to his enemy, and 'unseam'd him from the nave to the chaps'. And then he tells of a second battle so bloody that the combatants seemed as if they 'meant to bathe in reeking wounds'. What metaphors! What a dreadful image is that with which Lady Macbeth greets us almost as she enters, when she prays the spirits of cruelty so to thicken her blood that pity cannot flow along her veins! What pictures are those of the murderer appearing at the door of the banquetroom with Banquo's 'blood upon his face'; of Banquo himself 'with twenty trenched gashes on his head', or 'bloodbolter'd' and smiling in derision at his murderer; of Macbeth, gazing at his hand, and watching it dye the whole green ocean red; of Lady Macbeth, gazing at hers, and stretching it away from her face to escape the smell of blood that all the perfumes of Arabia will not subdue! The most horrible lines in the whole tragedy are those of her shuddering cry, 'Yet who would have thought the old man to have had so much blood in him?' And it is not only at such moments that these images occur. Even in the quiet conversation of Malcolm and Macduff, Macbeth is imagined as holding a bloody sceptre, and Scotland as a country bleeding and receiving every day a new gash added to her wounds. It is as if the poet saw the whole story through an ensanguined mist, and as if it stained the very blackness of the night. When Macbeth, before Banquo's murder, invokes night to scarf up the tender eye of pitiful day, and to tear in pieces the great bond that keeps him pale, even the invisible hand that is to tear the bond is imagined as covered with blood.

Let us observe another point. The vividness, magnitude, and violence of the imagery in some of these passages are characteristic of *Macbeth* almost throughout; and their influence contributes to form its atmosphere. Images like those of the babe torn smiling from the breast and dashed to death; of pouring the sweet milk of concord into hell; of the earth shaking in fever; of the frame of things disjointed; of sorrows striking heaven on the face, so that it resounds and yells out like syllables of dolour; of the mind lying in restless ecstasy on a rack; of the mind full of scorpions; of the tale told by an idiot, full of sound and fury; – all keep the imagination moving on a 'wild and violent sea', while it is scarcely for a moment permitted to dwell on thoughts of peace and beauty. In its language, as in its action, the drama is full of tumult and storm. . . .

In the 1930s the study of Shakespeare's imagery was boosted by the imagistic poetry then being written and was put on a more systematic basis by Caroline Spurgeon in *Shakespeare's Imagery and What It Tells Us* (1935). What she started as an enquiry into the workings of

Shakespeare's unconscious mind became a way of defining the imaginative sources and intellectual interests of individual plays, often
disclosing what is not verbally explicit. Having collected images of
ill-fitting clothing in *Macbeth*, Caroline Spurgeon argued that
Shakespeare presented its hero as 'a notably small man enveloped in
a coat far too big for him', citing Chaplin as an instance of a comic
actor who appreciated such an effect. Macbeth uses the image early
in the play – 'Why do you dress me / In borrowed robes?' (I.iii.107–8)
– and, soon afterwards, Banquo develops it:

> New honours come upon him
> Like our strange garments, cleave not to their mould
> But with the aid of use.

> (I.iii.144–6)

Echoes multiply, often in contexts where they suggest unlikely
visions: for example, 'Golden opinions . . . warn in their newest gloss'
and 'a giant's robe / Upon a dwarfish thief'. Caroline Spurgeon noted
two other series of images, that of sounds echoing and re-echoing in
the air and the more familiar one of light standing for life, virtue,
goodness; darkness for evil and death.

Other critics soon followed, bringing a still closer examination of
the text and a concern with intellectual meanings rather than mood
or tone. In 1947, Cleanth Brook asked in *The Well-wrought Urn* for the
same attention to be given to Shakespeare's verse as readers had
learnt to give to the quick-changing and playful nature of John
Donne's lyrics: if they did not do so they would fail to understand
either writer. When Macbeth compares the pity that will be given to
the king he is about to kill to a 'naked, new-born babe, / Striding the
blast' (I.vii.21–2), the oddity of the image led Cleanth Brooks to question whether that babe is:

> natural or supernatural – an ordinary, helpless baby, who, as newborn,
> could not, of course, even toddle, much less stride the blast? Or is it some
> infant Hercules, quite capable of striding the blast?

'Heaven's cherubim', which follows as an alternative image, supports
the latter alternative and prompts the further question: 'Does

Shakespeare mean for pity or for fear of retribution to be dominant in Macbeth's mind?' From these considerations, the critic procedes to look at the many other references to young infants in this play, sometimes real (for example, Macduff's 'pretty ones'), sometimes symbolic (for example, two of the apparitions raised by the Witches in Act IV, scene i), and sometimes metaphoric, as in this passage. The 'naked, newborn babe' is not merely an extravagant turn of phrase but also an encapsulation of the play's primary concern with lineal inheritance, childlessness, and infertility. After he has killed Duncan, babes again dominate Macbeth's thoughts: 'For Banquo's issue have I filed my mind, / For them, the gracious Duncan have I murdered' (III.i.59–60). It is neither his courage in defeat nor his great imagination that places Macbeth 'beside the other great tragic protagonists' but rather 'his attempt to conquer the future, an attempt involving him, like Oedipus, in a desperate struggle with fate itself'. Examination of one word has led this critic to a reassessment of the entire play.

William Empson in *The Structure of Complex Words* (1951) focused attention on single words still more sharply by studying them in a wider context. Having isolated several meanings of the word *fool* in *King Lear*, he brings this analysis to bear on Macbeth's speech immediately before confronting Macduff:

> Why should I play the Roman fool and die
> On mine own sword? Whiles I see lives, the gashes
> Do better upon them.
>
> (V.vi.40–2)

Empson can show that the sense 'lunatic clown' often 'pokes itself forward . . . where the context does not directly require it'. Along with *play* in the sense of 'perform', Macbeth seems to consider playing some kind of clown's part. We might add that the 'sword' becomes the fool's sceptre, the 'gashes' on other people the slashed colours of a clown's motley costume. Complex words and their multiple meanings have become an often-practised tool for assessing the 'hidden' structures of Shakespeare's plays: M. M. Mahood's *Shakespeare's Wordplay* (1957) provides excellent examples.

Rhetoric, syntax, versification and rhythm have also been studied as an aid to criticism. In 1985, Michael Goldman's *Acting and Action in Shakespearean Tragedy* (1985) had a chapter on 'Language and Action in *Macbeth*' which is attentive to sentence structure, rhythm, and sound, as well as the meanings of individual words. He notes, for example, the physical effect of a 'tongue-twister' and the 'disturbing density' of meanings in the first line of:

> This supernatural soliciting
> Cannot be ill, cannot be good.

(I.iii.129–30)

The Elizabethan meanings of *solicit* link together 'all kinds of persuasion – evil, neutral, and good; rhetorical, sexual, sympathetic, and manipulative'. As the speech continues, 'Balances are set up which are quickly undermined by unassimilated residues of sound and sense . . . a twisting and darkening, a thickening in which the speech thrusts forward into little thickets of sound and into reflections which don't allow the speculative movement to exit.' Theatre language is physical as well as aural and so Macbeth is considered here as a man using images in both ways: he can be said to 'explore and discover his new emotions . . . very much like an actor rehearsing a role'; he tries to discover 'a convincing capacity' for the act of being murderer and traitor.

## Characters

The persons of a Shakespeare play are usually the first topics of discussion after seeing a performance and, together with the story, were the primary interest of the earliest critics. Shakespeare was often praised for his knowledge of psychology, as in Dr Samuel Johnson's observation (1765): 'The augments by which Lady Macbeth persuades her husband to commit the murder, afford a proof of Shakespeare's knowledge of human nature.' In the Romantic period, critics followed the play's action more closely and considered in detail the reactions of the principal persons in a play. William Hazlitt's *Characters of Shakespeare's Plays* (1817) provides a vivid example:

Macbeth himself appears driven along by the violence of his fate like a vessel drifting before a storm: he reels to and fro like a drunken man; he staggers under the weight of his own purposes and the suggestions of others; he stands at bay with his situation; and from the superstitious awe and breathless suspense into which the communications of the Weird Sisters throw him, is hurried on with daring impatience to verify their predictions, and with impious and bloody hand to tear aside the veil which hides the uncertainty of the future. He is not equal to the struggle with fate and conscience. . . . In thought he is absent and perplexed, sudden and desperate in act, from distrust of his own resolution. His energy springs from the anxiety and agitation of his mind.

A. C. Bradley's *Shakespearean Tragedy* (1904) gave motivation a more sustained and critical consideration than any previous study through a constant concern for the 'greatness' and moral qualities of the tragic heroes and an ability to relate detailed observation to the development of whole plays. The following excerpt from his account of Lady Macbeth illustrates his attention to contrasts and other features of play construction:

To regard *Macbeth* as a play, like the love-tragedies *Romeo and Juliet* and *Antony and Cleopatra*, in which there are two central characters of equal importance, is certainly a mistake. But Shakespeare himself is in a measure responsible for it, because the first half of *Macbeth* is greater than the second, and in the first half Lady Macbeth not only appears more than in the second but exerts the ultimate deciding influence on the action. And, in the opening Act at least, Lady Macbeth is the most commanding and perhaps the most awe-inspiring figure that Shakespeare drew. Sharing, as we have seen, certain traits with her husband, she is at once clearly distinguished from him by an inflexibility of will, which appears to hold imagination, feeling, and conscience completely in check. To her the prophecy of things that will be becomes instantaneously the determination that they shall be:

> Glamis thou art, and Cawdor, and shalt be
> What thou art promised.

She knows her husband's weakness, how he scruples 'to catch the nearest way' to the object he desires; and she sets herself without a trace of doubt or conflict to counteract this weakness. To her there is no separation between will and deed; and, as the deed falls in part to her, she is sure it will be done:

> The raven himself is hoarse
> That croaks the fatal entrance of Duncan
> Under my battlements.

On the moment of Macbeth's rejoining her, after braving infinite dangers and winning infinite praise, without a syllable on these subjects or a word of affection, she goes straight to her purpose and permits him to speak of nothing else. She takes the superior position and assumes the direction of affairs, – appears to assume it even more than she really can, that she may spur him on. She animates him by picturing the deed as heroic, 'this night's *great* business', or 'our *great* quell', while she ignores its cruelty and faithlessness. She bears down his faint resistance by presenting him with a prepared scheme which may remove from him the terror and danger of deliberation. She rouses him with a taunt no man can bear, and least of all a soldier, – the word 'coward'. She appeals even to his love for her:

> from this time
> Such I account thy love;

– such, that is, as the protestations of a drunkard. Her reasonings are mere sophisms; they could persuade no man. It is not by them, it is by personal appeals, through the admiration she extorts from him, and through sheer force of will, that she impels him to the deed. Her eyes are fixed upon the crown and the means to it; she does not attend to the consequences. Her plan of laying the guilt upon the chamberlains is invented on the spur of the moment, and simply to satisfy her husband. Her true mind is heard in the ringing cry with which she answers his question, 'Will it not be received . . . that they have done it?'

> Who *dares* receive it other?

And this is repeated in the sleepwalking scene: 'What need we fear who knows it, when none can call our power to account?' Her passionate courage sweeps him off his feet. His decision is taken in a moment of enthusiasm:

> Bring forth menchildren only;
> For thy undaunted mettle should compose
> Nothing but males.

And even when passion has quite died away her will remains supreme. In presence of overwhelming horror and danger, in the murder scene and the banquet scene, her selfcontrol is perfect. When the truth of what she has done dawns on her, no word of complaint, scarcely a word of her own suffering, not a single word of her own as apart from his, escapes her when others are by. She helps him, but never asks his help. She leans on nothing but herself. And from the beginning to the end – though she makes once or twice a slip in acting her part – her will never fails her. Its grasp upon her nature may destroy her, but it is never relaxed. . . .

Bradley was ready, like an actor is, to imagine the action of the play continuing beneath and beyond what is said:

the development of her character – perhaps it would be more strictly accurate to say, the change in her state of mind – is both inevitable, and the opposite of the development we traced in Macbeth. When the murder has been done, the discovery of its hideousness, first reflected in the faces of her guests, comes to Lady Macbeth with the shock of a sudden disclosure, and at once her nature begins to sink. The first intimation of the change is given when, in the scene of the discovery, she faints. When next we see her, Queen of Scotland, the glory of her dream has faded. She enters, disillusioned, and weary with want of sleep: she has thrown away everything and gained nothing:

> Nought's had, all's spent,
> Where our desire is got without content:
> 'Tis safer to be that which we destroy
> Than by destruction dwell in doubtful joy.

Henceforth she has no initiative: the stem of her being seems to be cut through. Her husband, physically the stronger, maddened by pangs he had foreseen, but still flaming with life, comes into the foreground, and she retires. Her will remains, and she does her best to help him; but he rarely needs her help. Her chief anxiety appears to be that he should not betray his misery. He plans the murder of Banquo without her knowledge (not in order to spare her, I think, for he never shows love of this quality, but merely because he does not need her now); and even when she is told vaguely of his intention she appears but little interested. In the sudden emergency of the banquet scene she makes a prodigious and magnificent effort; her strength, and with it her ascendancy, returns, and she saves her husband at least from an open disclosure. But after this she takes no part whatever in the action. We only know from her shuddering words in the sleep-walking scene, 'The Thane of Fife had a wife: where is she now?' that she has even learned of her husband's worst crime; and in all the horrors of his tyranny over Scotland she has, so far as we hear, no part. Disillusionment and despair prey upon her more and more. That she should seek any relief in speech, or should ask for sympathy, would seem to her mere weakness, and would be to Macbeth's defiant fury an irritation. Thinking of the change in him, we imagine the bond between them slackened, and Lady Macbeth left much alone. She sinks slowly downward. She cannot bear darkness, and has light by her continually: 'tis her command. At last her nature, not her will, gives way. The secrets of the past find vent in a disorder of sleep, the beginning perhaps of madness. What the doctor fears is clear. He reports to her husband no great physical mischief, but bids her attendant to remove from her all means by which she could harm herself, and to keep eyes on her constantly. It is in vain. Her death is announced by a cry from her women so sudden and direful that it would thrill her husband with horror if he were any longer capable of fear. In the last words of the play Malcolm tells us it is believed in the hostile army that she died by her own hand . . . it is in accordance with her character that even in her weakest hour she should cut short by one determined stroke the agony of her life.

Bradley's involvement with the details of the text and action is impressively thorough and will send many readers back to the play to keep up with his discourse. In later criticism the study of Shakespeare's characters would often move into still wider territory beyond the words of the text. An example pre-dating Bradley, is Coleridge's comment on Lady Macbeth's intention to 'chastise' her husband 'with the valour of my tongue' (I.v.25), which refers to her social milieu. Belonging to a class of high rank,

> left much alone, and feeding herself with day dreams of ambition, she mistakes the courage of fantasy for the power of bearing the consequences of the realities of guilt. Hers is the mock fortitude of a mind

deluded by ambition; she shames her husband with a superhuman audacity of fancy which she cannot support, but sinks in the season of remorse, and dies in suicidal agony.

Imagining Shakespeare's characters in more familiar circumstances than that of the plays was a conspicuous tendency in the nineteenth century that led to assessments that were moral or general in relevance. They were frequently expressions of the critic's own personal experiences and interests: for example, Anna Jameson's *Shakespeare's Heroines: Characteristics of Women, Moral, Poetical and Historical* (1832).

In later years the apparent life-likeness of the *dramatis personae* encouraged comparisons with characters in nineteenth-century novels and famous plays. For example, from Robert Ornstein's *The Moral Vision of Jacobean Tragedy* (1960):

> If we applaud Dostoevski's understanding of the psychopathology of crime, must we not also applaud Shakespeare's portrait of Macbeth, who like Raskolnikov commits a crime that revolts him ... who like Raskolnikov walks towards the deed as in a trance, scarce believing that he can commit the act that fortune has cast in his way?

Both heroes kill for peace in their own minds, 'to end the restless torment' of their imaginations. Norman Rabkin in *Shakespeare and the Problem of Meaning* (1981) drew parallels with the myth of Oedipus to explain Macbeth's reference to 'The expedition of my violent love' (II.iii.117) when he speaks of coming within sight of Duncan, the royal father whom he has killed. He also points out that 'it is the very act of treating Malcolm as a favorite son that triggers a murderous impulse' in Macbeth's mind, together with an acknowledgement of 'my black and deep desires' (see I.iv.49–54). Shakespeare knew nothing directly of Greek tragedy and nothing at all of Freudian psychology but critics have used both to understand and judge the persons of this and other plays.

In recent years more frequent use has been made of psychic myths of origin and psychoanalysis, often in association with gender studies. *Macbeth* lacks a dominant mother-figure but Janet Adelman's *Suffocating Mothers: Fantasies of Maternal Origin in Shakespeare's plays, 'Hamlet' to 'The Tempest'* (1992) argues that the influence of one is:

diffused throughout the play, evoked primarily by the figures of the witches and Lady Macbeth . . . the play becomes (like *Coriolanus*) a representation of primitive fears about male identity and autonomy itself, about those looming female presences who threaten to control one's actions and one's mind, to constitute one's very self, even at a distance.

Language is crucial to establishing this argument: for example, when Macbeth is said to carve out his passage to Macdonwald 'with his brandished steel', he does so after 'Disdaining Fortune' who has 'showed like a rebel's whore' (I.ii.8–20), that is, metaphorically, 'carving his passage through a female body'. When Ross tells Malcolm that Scotland 'cannot / Be called our mother, but our grave', Janet Adelman comments that 'it is the realm of Lady Macbeth and the witches, the realm in which the mother *is* the grave, the realm appropriately ruled by their bad son Macbeth'. From the outward marks of individuality the study of character has reached far underneath the text and into general and wider implications of what they do.

## Arguments, themes and meanings

Claudius, Prince Hal and King Henry the Fourth all speak of the action of a play or of a reign as presenting an 'argument' (*Hamlet*, III.ii.221, *1 Henry IV*, II.v.284–5, and *2 Henry IV*, IV.iii.326–7), a word that today is likely to be replaced by *theme* or *meaning*. All three words have been used by critics when considering the overall impression that a play makes on the minds of an audience or reader.

Until comparatively recently most thematic analyses of *Macbeth* identified a moral argument. Helen Gardner's influential essay in *English Studies, 1948* compares the play with Christopher Marlowe's *Dr Faustus*, stating very simply that 'the theme of damnation was explicit for Marlowe' and that 'Shakespeare reads it into the story of Macbeth, or rather he shapes his material to bring out the same fundamental conceptions as are embodied in the Faustus myth.' The introduction of Young Seyward is to show how 'God's soldier' dies (V.vi.86), the opposite to the 'brave' and 'so valiant' Macbeth (I.ii.16 and I.iv.55) who at the end of the play 'is simply a wild beast to be destroyed'. A few

years earlier Theodore Spencer's *Shakespeare and the Nature of Man*
(1943) had called *Macbeth* a 'more intense study of evil than any other
[of Shakespeare's plays]. Unlike *King Lear*, this tragedy portrays, not
the whitening, but the blackening of a soul.' But with more space to
elaborate, the argument is not so starkly described here: in Malcolm
there is 'a promise of ultimate good' and the cause of evil is uncertain:

> We never know, as we see or read *Macbeth*, whether the weird sisters
> control Macbeth's fate, or whether their prophecies are a reflection of
> Macbeth's own character. The problem of predestination and free-will is
> present, but is left unanswered.

Other critics have used scholarly investigation to decipher the play's
argument. Accepting contemporary beliefs that witches could be
agents of the devil or demons with influence on human lives, W. C.
Curry, in *Shakespeare's Philosophical Patterns* (1937), and Garry Wills, in
*Witches and Jesuits* (1995), have read the tragedy as a struggle for
Macbeth's soul. According to Garry Wills, a supernatural charm is
wound around him in Act IV, scene i, that is broken only when
Macduff fights him off stage in the final scene; when he returns, as the
Folio directs, he has become 'assailable' (III.ii.39) like other mortals. But
the beliefs about witches that these critics presented were not univer-
sally held and Shakespeare's use of them is far more ambiguous than
they acknowledge (see pp. 20 and 24 above and pp. 159–60 below).

More certain grounds for identifying themes and meanings have
been found in the text's mythical references and the story's associations with folklore and customs. In a series of books, G. Wilson
Knight considered certain words as recurrent symbols that expressed
the play's meanings. His *Shakespearian Tempest* (1932) provided a chart
with which to identify the symbolic force of recurrent words and
from these he deduced that tempests of various and violent kinds
define the form and, therefore, the argument of *Macbeth*: 'chaos,
disintegration, and death embattled against degree and order . . .
hospitality, love and life'. These symbols were present visually in the
Apparitions scene (IV.i): the armed Head is a 'death-symbol', the
bloody Child a symbol of 'Life-born-out-of-death', and the Child
crowned, with a tree in his hand, a symbol 'of Life victorious, its

"baby-brow" imperially crowned with the golden circlet of Nature's innocence, its little hand sceptred with the Tree of Life'. Wilson Knight calls the apparitions a 'whole miniature drama suggesting a conflict, each apparition comes with thunder . . . – the thunderous shock of Life and Death opposed'.

John Holloway in *The Story of the Night* (1961) looks for symbolic action in the story of the play rather than in recurrent words, and these he identifies by reference to folk customs and biblical traditions. He says that the image of the bloody man, that other critics have noticed in the opening scenes of *Macbeth*, is more than an image: 'It is an apparition. It haunts the stage.' And more than an image of death; it is 'the Great Doom's image' that Macduff recognizes as he looks upon Duncan's murdered body (II.iii.75). Macbeth's speech on returning to the Witches in Act IV, scene i, he sees as an act as well as speech, a 'ritualized invocation of universal disaster on Nature in pursuit of his own ends'. At the end, the king is:

> driven out and destroyed by the forces which embody the fertile vitality and the communal happiness of the social group. . . . The element of ritual in the closing scenes, their almost imperceptible relapsing into the contours of a sacrificial fertility ceremony, the expulsion, hunting down and destruction of man who has turned into a monster, give to the action its final shape.

L. C. Knights, in *Some Shakespearean Themes* (1959), identifies much the same line of argument as Holloway and Wilson Knight but locates it in a social and historical setting. He brings into the foreground of his argument Macbeth's words after seeing Banquo's ghost:

> Blood hath been shed ere now, i'the olden time,
> Ere humane statute purged the gentle weal . . .
>
> (III.iv.74–5)

Macbeth's killing, he comments, is 'a violation of his essential humanity'. The recurring words that he notices are not descriptive of tempests, light, or angels but active ones denoting human relationships: *concord, peace, unity, children, servants, guest, host, duties.*

Considering these issues throughout the play, Knights envisages Shakespeare as a social thinker and troubled intellectual: 'we have in this play an answer to Shakespeare's earlier questionings about time's power'. Macbeth has 'turned his back on, has indeed attempted violence on, those values that alone give significance to duration'.

Another group of critics have brought their own contemporary interests to a study of the play and found reflections of them in its text, especially in those elements which challenge established authorities and the principles upon which their power is based. In its brief account of *Macbeth*, Jonathan Dollimore's *Radical Tragedy: Religion, Ideology and Power in the Drama of Shakespeare and his Contemporaries* (1984) focuses on the two Murderers as victims of the society in which they live, who lack any means to mend their lives: one is 'reckless what / I do to spite the world', the other willing to 'set my life on any chance, / To mend it or be rid on't' (III.i.107–13). Extreme poverty has rendered these men fit accomplices for Macbeth; they are the fellows to whom he must turn before presiding in the 'great feast' that celebrates his kingship.

Concern for outsiders and the disadvantaged led several of the 'cultural Materialist' critics to pay special attention to the Witches. Terry Eagleton, in his *Shakespeare* of 1986, accompanies his section on *Macbeth* with a quotation from the *Communist Manifesto*, in much the same way as recent character studies establish their credentials by quoting Freud or his successors. In the bourgeois epoch, according to Marx and Engels, 'All that is solid melts into air, all that is holy is profaned, and man is at last compelled to face with sober senses his real conditions of life, and his relations with his kind.' For Terry Eagleton, the Witches are the heroines of the play, even though this is scarcely recognized in the text and has been given little space in the structure of the play:

> It is they who, by releasing ambitious thoughts in Macbeth, expose a reverence for hierarchical social order for what it is, as the pious self-deception of a society based on routine oppression and incessant warfare. The witches are exiles from that violent order, inhabiting their own sisterly community on its shadowy borderlands, refusing all truck with its tribal bickerings and military honours.

In effect, this critic argues, Macbeth's encounters with the Witches release his lust for power, which the play condemns as evil or 'foul' but was natural to its world of cut-throat rivalry between noblemen.

In an essay published in *Focus on 'Macbeth'* (1982), Peter Stallybrass found evidence for a rather different view by looking carefully in the text and into contemporary beliefs about witchcraft. Noting that Shakespeare had rejected Holinshed's suggestion that the witches might be 'the goddesses of destiny' (see p. 105 above), he argued that 'Only by making his Sisters forces of darkness could Shakespeare suggest demonic opposition to godly rule . . . both the Witches and Macbeth threaten to bring the world back to its first chaos.' A biblical quotation, much used in treatises on witchcraft, underlined the connection: 'For Rebellion is as the sin of witchcraft' (1 Samuel, XV, 23). In this view, the Witches represent female rule and the overthrow of patriarchal authority, the killing of the 'holy' father, and the destruction of family.

## Structure, action and genre

The early adaptations of the text and the first extended criticisms agreed in accounting *Macbeth* 'irregular' and yet, at much the same time, the tragedy was considered a masterpiece (see above, p. 144). In the essay already quoted (pp. 150–1, above), Hazlitt offered a considered vindication of the play's structure and an explanation of its success with audiences and readers:

> *Macbeth* (generally speaking) is done upon a stronger and more system-atic principle of contrast than any other of Shakespeare's plays. It moves upon the verge of an abyss, and is a constant struggle between life and death. The action is desperate and the reaction is dreadful. It is a huddling together of fierce extremes, a war of opposite natures which of them shall destroy the other. There is nothing but what has a violent end or violent beginnings. The lights and shades are laid on with a determined hand; the transitions from triumph to despair, from the height of terror to the repose of death, are sudden and startling; every passion brings in its fellow-contrary, and the thoughts pitch and jostle against each other as in the dark. The whole play is an unruly chaos of strange and forbidden

things, where the ground rocks under our feet. Shakespeare's genius here took its full swing, and trod upon the furthest bounds of nature and passion. This circumstance will account for the abruptness and violent antitheses of the style, the throes and labour which run through the expression, and from defects will turn them into beauties.

Later critics have seen the origin of *Macbeth*'s structure in Miracle and early narrative plays of an English native tradition, and in Shakespeare's own history plays, rather than in the more formal shaping of tragedies derived from Seneca and, ultimately, from the Greeks. The criticism of Helen Gardner and John Holloway are examples of this, accepting that the play is concerned with process rather than a single crisis and clash of opposites.

More recently, the spectacular elements and use of music in *Macbeth*, which have similarities to the court masques of the time and incidents in Shakespeare's later romances, have led some critics to see the play as a baroque construction. The most enthusiastic proponent of this view has been Nicholas Brooke in his Introduction and annotations to the Oxford edition (1990). By calling the tragedy a 'Baroque drama' and recognizing the part that wonder and amazement play in its reception, this critic willingly accepts and seeks to justify the 'sensational credulity' that the play seems to demand of an audience and which imagistic, thematic, and character-centred criticism tends to sidestep or ignore:

> Its dramatic form . . . depends upon a spectrum of dramatic illusions which are set in unusually sharp contrast with the naturalism invested in the Macbeths' relationship. The result is a sharp dichotomy between realism and supernatural phenomena. Neither is viewed simply . . .

Macbeth and his wife are seen by others in epic and grand terms: at first he is valorous and she gracious; later they are a bloody butcher and a fiend-like queen. Yet to readers and audience, through their soliloquies and asides, they are sensitive, acute, pained and puzzled. The supernatural is also presented ambivalently, 'an invitation to credulity' being off-set by 'an inclination towards scepticism'. These are 'precisely the terms', comments Nicholas Brooke, 'that I would use about the aesthetic structures of Roman baroque art in the first half of the seventeenth century'.

In an article of 1999, '*Macbeth* and the Antic Round', Stephen Orgel made much the same point, arguing that the elaboration of the Witches' songs and dances in early productions showed that the masque elements of the play were more acceptable and more meaningful than they have seemed to many later critics: 'the first thing they do for this claustrophobic play is to open a space for women; and it is a subversive and paradoxical space'.

## Theatrical events

*Macbeth* is one of the most frequently performed of Shakespeare's plays and yet one whose success is far from certain. Reviewers frequently disapprove and some of the most talented and experienced actors have been defeated by the central role, Peter O'Toole and Ralph Richardson among them. For critics of the Romantic period, the play threatened to become too painful, as Charles Lamb wrote in 1811:

> The state of sublime emotion into which we are elevated by those images of night and horror which Macbeth is made to utter, that solemn prelude with which he entertains the time till the bell shall strike which is to call him to murder Duncan, – when we no longer read it in a book, when we have given up that vantage-ground of abstraction which reading possesses over seeing, and come to see a man in his bodily shape before our eyes actually preparing to commit a murder, if the acting be true and impressive, as I have witnessed it in Mr K[ean]'s performance of that part, the painful anxiety about the act, the natural longing to prevent it while it yet seems unperpetrated, the too close pressing semblance of reality, give a pain and an uneasiness which totally destroy all the delight which the words in the book convey, where the deed-doing never presses upon us with the painful sense of presence. . . . The sublime images, the poetry alone, is that which is present to our minds in the reading.

For William Hazlitt, the play had no chance of working in the theatre:

> We can conceive no one to play Macbeth properly, or to look like a man that had encountered the Weird sisters. All the actors that we have ever

seen, appear as if they had encountered them on the boards of Covent Garden or Drury Lane, but not on the heath at Fores, and as if they did not believe what they had seen. The witches of *Macbeth* indeed are ridiculous on the modern stage, and we doubt if the furies of Aeschylus would be more respected.

These problems have not gone away with time. As we have seen, Professors Brooke and Orgel have argued that the tragedy combines two modes of presentation, one of which is against present-day theatrical conventions, and the two seeming irreconcilable with each other. Stark Young reviewing a production at the Knickerbocker Theatre, New York, in 1928 identified the problem as that of 'a primitive and barbaric history done over into seventeenth century matter'; and neither element belongs to our culture: we 'cannot quite receive the play as one harmonious unity in kind'. He also complained that 'realism' could not accommodate the play's 'poetic method'. To speak Macbeth's lines about 'innocent sleep' (II.ii.36–40) with breaks in them, as if one thought arose after another, 'is only to make the character sound rambling or irrelevant to the dramatic moment and truth, and the dramatist more or less talky or false'.

But the chapter above, on 'Key Productions and Performances', shows that these difficulties can be overcome. In the *Sunday Times*, John Peter's review of a 1999 production faulted it for not realizing that 'some of its most crucial scenes' have to be 'terrifyingly' intimate: action, spectacle, and clear, eloquent, and poetic speaking are not enough to carry the drama: it must also be painful and frightening. Writing for *The Times* in 2004, Benedict Nightingale reported that the latest Macbeth, an actor 'with many fine qualities', had been found wanting. The more this highly experienced reviewer sees *Macbeth*, the more sure he becomes that two demands must be met if the play is to fulfil the promise it has on the page:

> One is a theatre small enough for the audience, like the protagonist, to feel that it's on agonisingly intimate terms with evil. The other is a Macbeth with darkness and danger not just in his mind and heart but in his stomach and bowels.

# Further Reading

## I   The text and first performance

### (i)   Editions

Recent editions of the play, with scholarly introductions, annotations and textual collations, are by Nicholas Brooke (Oxford: Oxford University Press, 1990) and A. R. Braunmuller (Cambridge: Cambridge University Press, 1997). The New Penguin edition, first published in 1965 and updated 1995, is competitively priced and easy to use; quotations and references in this *Handbook* are taken from this book. Other inexpensive editions of the play that are available throughout the world are in the Pelican, Signet, and Folger series.

### (ii)   Theatre history and theatre practice

Authority for the factual information in Chapter 1 will be found in the following books and in the Oxford and Cambridge editions cited above.

J. Leeds Barroll, *Politics, Plague, and Shakespeare's Theater* (1991), pp. 133–52, offers an alternative view of the dating and occasion of the first performance of *Macbeth*.

Andrew Gurr, *The Shakespearean Stage, 1574–1642*, 3rd edn (Cambridge: Cambridge University Press, 1992), a thoroughly responsible account of what is known about the theatrical conditions in which Shakespeare's plays were first performed.

Peter Thomson, *Shakespeare's Theatre* (London: Routledge & Kegan Paul, 1983); includes a chapter on '*Macbeth* from the tiring house'.

## II    General studies

Stephen Booth, *'King Lear', 'Macbeth', Indefinition, and Tragedy* (New Haven and London: Yale University Press, 1983).

A. C. Bradley, *Shakespearean Tragedy: Lectures on 'Hamlet', 'Othello', 'King Lear', 'Macbeth'* (London: Macmillan, 1904, and constantly in print).

John Russell Brown, *Shakespeare: The Tragedies* (London and New York: Palgrave Macmillan, 2001), its similarity in outlook recommends this book to readers who wish to proceed from a study of *Macbeth* to Shakespeare's other tragedies.

John Russell Brown (ed.), *Focus on 'Macbeth'* (London: Routledge & Kegan Paul, 1982), a collection of specially commissioned essays on the themes, structure and performance of the play, which include Peter Stallybrass's essay on witchcraft and another by the historian Michael Hawkins, on the play's political context.

Stephen Orgel, *Imagining Shakespeare* (London and New York: Palgrave Macmillan, 2003).

## III    Sources and context

### (i)    Witches

Frederick Kiefer, *Shakespeare's Visual Theatre* (Cambridge: Cambridge University Press, 2003), discusses and illustrates the appearance of Hecate and witches in *Macbeth* and other publications of its time.

Barbara Rosen (ed.), *Witchcraft* (London: Arnold, 1968), although long out of print, is an edited anthology of pamphlets on the subject from the sixteenth and seventeenth centuries that is well worth seeking out.

Keith Thomas, *Religion and the Decline of Magic* (London: Weidenfeld and Nicolson, 1971), includes a wide-ranging and judicious account of witchcraft in Britain.

Gary Wills, *Witches and Jesuits: Shakespeare's 'Macbeth'* (New York and Cambridge: New York Public Library and Cambridge University Press, 1995), an account of the play that gives full credence to the witches' supernatural powers and the effectiveness of their rituals.

## (ii)    *Kingship and politics*

The Cambridge edition of the play, by A. R. Braunmuller (1997), gives
    a full account of recent scholarship on the play's sources and
    political and social context.

Jonathan Goldberg, *James I and the Politics of Literature* (Stanford, CA:
    Stanford University Press, 1983).

Steven Mullaney, *The Place of the Stage* (Chicago: University of Chicago
    Press, 1988), an account of the cultural and topographical contexts
    of Elizabethan and Jacobean theatres.


See also *Focus on Macbeth* in the General Section, above.


## IV    The play in production and performance

Dennis Bartholomeusz, *'Macbeth' and the Players* (Cambridge:
    Cambridge University Press, 1969); its broad scope and documen-
    tation will long be valuable despite too great a reverence for the
    Folio's punctuation.

Michael R. Booth and others, *Three Tragic Actresses: Siddons, Rachel,
    Ristori* (Cambridge: Cambridge University Press, 1996), contains a
    judicious account of Sarah Siddons's Lady Macbeth that is
    supported by generous documentation.

Alan Hughes, *Henry Irving, Shakespearean* (Cambridge: Cambridge
    University Press, 1981), contains a carefully researched account of
    Irving's Macbeth that is informed by a knowledge of theatre practice.

Bernice W. Kilman, *'Macbeth': Shakespeare in Performance* (Manchester:
    Manchester University Press, 2nd edition, 2003); after a historical
    introduction, this account of individual productions gives most
    attention to those that could be seen in recent years in North
    America and to film versions.

Michael Mullin, *'Macbeth' on Stage* (Columbia, MI, and London:
    University of Missouri Press, 1976), contains a facsimile of Glen
    Byam Shaw's promptbook for his 1955 production with Laurence
    Olivier in the lead; it has many illustrations and is copiously anno-
    tated from numerous sources.

Marvin Rosenberg, *The Masks of Macbeth* (Berkeley and London: University of California Press, 1978), presents many descriptions of how the text has been played in a wide range of productions over many years and in several countries. Following the play scene by scene, it is too detailed to read from cover to cover and is of little help in the study of any particular production or performance. Its main use is as a treasure trove for anyone wanting to know how any single line has been acted by leading actors.

John Wilders (ed.), *'Macbeth': Shakespeare in Production* (Cambridge: Cambridge University Press, 2004), an edition of the play with extensive notes, giving details about staging and performance in numerous productions and recording all the deletions and modifications that were made.

Reviews of British productions since 1981 are collected and republished in the periodical *Theatre Record*.

## V   Film, video and audio versions

Because recordings are liable to be offered in varying formats with new reference numbers, only titles and directors' names are given here together with the original issue date; from this information, the latest and most convenient reissue can be identified.

### (i)   *Films described in this Handbook*

*The Throne of Blood*, a film by Akira Kurosawa, Japan, 1957; Japanese language with English subtitles.

*Macbeth*, directed by Roman Polanski; 'Screenplay by Roman Polanski and Kenneth Tynan, from the play by William Shakespeare,' 1971.

*Macbeth*, A Royal Shakespeare Company performance, produced by Trevor Nunn, 1978.

## (ii)    *Other available films and videos*

*Macbeth*, directed by Orson Welles, 1936.

*Macbeth*, directed by Jack Gold, 1982.

*Macbeth*, directed by Yukio Ninagawa, in Japanese with no subtitles, 1985.

*Macbeth*, directed by Gregory Doran, 2001.

## (iii)    *Audio recordings*

*Macbeth*, directed by George Rylands, with members of the Marlowe Society, Cambridge, 1959.

*Macbeth*, directed by Richard Eyre, with Ken Stott and Phyllis Logan, 2000.

*Macbeth*, with Hugh Rose and Harriet Walter, not dated.

*Macbeth*, with Stephan Dillane and Fiona Shaw, 1998.

## VI    Critical assessments

### *Books quoted in the Handbook*

Janet Adelman, *Suffocating Mothers: Fantasies of Maternal Origin in Shakespeare's Plays, 'Hamlet' to 'The Tempest'* (London and New York: Routledge, 1992).

Cleanth Brooks, *The Well-wrought Urn* (New York: Harcourt Brace, 1947).

Jonathan Dollimore, *Radical Tragedy: Religion, Ideology and Power in the Drama of Shakespeare and his Contemporaries*, 3rd edn (London and New York: Duke University Press, 2003).

Terry Eagleton, *Shakespeare* (Oxford: Blackwell, 1986).

William Empson, *The Structure of Complex Words* (London: Chatto & Windus, 3rd edition, 1977).

Michael Goldman, *Acting and Action in Shakespearean Tragedy* (Princeton, NJ: Princeton University Press, 1985).

John Holloway, *The Story of the Night: Studies in Shakespeare's Major Tragedies* (London: Routledge & Kegan Paul, 1961).

L. C. Knights, *Some Shakespearean Themes* (London: Chatto & Windus, 1959).

M. M. Mahood, *Shakespeare's Wordplay* (London: Methuen, 1957).

Stephen Orgel, 'Macbeth and the Antic Round', *Shakespeare Survey*, 53 (Cambridge: Cambridge University Press, 1999), pp. 143–53.

Robert Ornstein, *The Moral Vision of Jacobean Tragedy* (Madison: University of Wisconsin Press, 1960).

Norman Rabkin, *Shakespeare and the Problem of Meaning* (Chicago: University of Chicago Press, 1981).

Theodore Spencer, *Shakespeare and the Nature of Man* (Cambridge: Cambridge University Press, 1943).

Caroline Spurgeon, *Shakespeare's Imagery and What It Tells Us* (Cambridge: Cambridge University Press, 1935, and often reprinted).

G. Wilson Knight, *The Shakespearian Tempest*, 3rd edn (London: Methuen, 1953).

# Index